S0-BNT-403

Praise for the novels of John Shannon

"Like Graham Greene—and there are other admirable resemblances—he is an explorer of that shadowy area in which, as spurs to positive action, abstract idealism and personal psychology merge. The author has achieved one of the most stimulating of the form's uncountable possibilities." —*Sunday Times* (London)

"A serious adventure . . . [that] draws much of its strength from a clear presentation of social and political tensions." —*Times Literary Supplement*

"Fast and exciting action." —*Daily Telegraph* (London)

"Racy, ambitious." —Nancy Sigal

MORE MYSTERIES FROM THE
BERKLEY PUBLISHING GROUP...

DEWEY JAMES MYSTERIES: America's favorite small-town sleuth! "Highly entertaining!"   —*Booklist*

by Kate Morgan
A SLAY AT THE RACES   MYSTERY LOVES COMPANY
A MURDER MOST FOWL   DAYS OF CRIME AND ROSES
HOME SWEET HOMICIDE   THE OLD SCHOOL DIES

FORREST EVERS MYSTERIES: A former race-car driver solves the high-speed crimes of world-class racing... "A Dick Francis on wheels!"   —Jackie Stewart

by Bob Judd
BURN   SPIN
CURVE

THE REVEREND LUCAS HOLT MYSTERIES: They call him "The Rev," a name he earned as pastor of a Texas prison. Now he solves crimes with a group of reformed ex-cons...

by Charles Meyer
THE SAINTS OF GOD MURDERS   BLESSED ARE THE MERCILESS

FRED VICKERY MYSTERIES: Senior sleuth Fred Vickery has been around long enough to know where the bodies are buried in the small town of Cutler, Colorado...

by Sherry Lewis
NO PLACE FOR SECRETS   NO PLACE LIKE HOME
NO PLACE FOR DEATH   NO PLACE FOR TEARS
NO PLACE FOR SIN

INSPECTOR BANKS MYSTERIES: Award-winning British detective fiction at its finest... "Robinson's novels are habit-forming!"   —*West Coast Review of Books*

by Peter Robinson
THE HANGING VALLEY   PAST REASON HATED
WEDNESDAY'S CHILD   FINAL ACCOUNT
GALLOWS VIEW   INNOCENT GRAVES

JACK McMORROW MYSTERIES: The highly acclaimed series set in a Maine mill town and starring a newspaperman with a knack for crime solving... "Gerry Boyle is the genuine article."   —Robert B. Parker

by Gerry Boyle
DEADLINE   BLOODLINE
LIFELINE   POTSHOT

SCOTLAND YARD MYSTERIES: Featuring Detective Superintendent Duncan Kincaid and his partner, Sergeant Gemma James ... "Charming!"   —*New York Times Book Review*

by Deborah Crombie
A SHARE IN DEATH   ALL SHALL BE WELL
LEAVE THE GRAVE GREEN   MOURN NOT YOUR DEAD

JOE WILDER MYSTERIES: Featuring struggling-novelist-turned detective Joe Wilder ... "Crime fiction at its riveting best."   —Faye Kellerman

by T.J. Phillips
DANCE OF THE MONGOOSE   WOMAN IN THE DARK

THE CONCRETE RIVER

JOHN SHANNON

BERKLEY PRIME CRIME, NEW YORK

If you purchased this book without a cover, you should be aware that
this book is stolen property. It was reported as ''unsold and destroyed''
to the publisher, and neither the author nor the publisher has received
any payment for this ''stripped book.''

THE CONCRETE RIVER

A Berkley Prime Crime Book / published by arrangement with
the author

PRINTING HISTORY
John Brown Books hardcover edition / 1996
Berkley Prime Crime mass-market edition / February 1998

All rights reserved.
Copyright © 1996 by John Shannon.
This book may not be reproduced in whole or in part,
by mimeograph or any other means, without permission.
For information address:
The Berkley Publishing Group, a member of Penguin Putnam Inc.,
200 Madison Avenue, New York, NY 10016.

The Putnam Berkley World Wide Web site address is
http://www.berkley.com

ISBN: 0-425-16193-5

Berkley Prime Crime Books are published
by The Berkley Publishing Group, a member of Penguin Putnam Inc.,
200 Madison Avenue, New York, NY 10016.
The name BERKLEY PRIME CRIME and the BERKLEY PRIME CRIME
design are trademarks belonging to Berkley Publishing Corporation.

PRINTED IN THE UNITED STATES OF AMERICA

10 9 8 7 6 5 4 3 2 1

For Sarah

The flat plains are indeed the
heartlands of the city's Id.

—Reyner Banham

THE CONCRETE RIVER

INCOMING

"ALLS I'M SAYING, WHEN IT SLOW LIKE THIS WEEK, WE got a *situation.*" Ducks slapped his palms, as if wiping away something unpleasant.

"You gonna quit bottles, man, get into weight?"

Li'l Hammer kicked his heels against the low brick wall in front of the empty industrial buildings where they sat. It was after two a.m. and no one on earth seemed to be buying.

"Hey, why not?"

"You ain't got the props. The bangers see you, you ain't gonna have no ass left on you at all."

"Fuck *that,*" Ducks said contemptuously, and he hunched his shoulders briefly, the mannerism that many people thought gave him his name, but Li'l Hammer had grown up with him and knew better.

"Hey, rain," Li'l Hammer said.

They both looked up at the dark clouds and then Ducks' eye went to the crumpled brown Ralphs bag, apparently discarded by the Walker Valve sign twenty yards away. They didn't sell anything from that bag locally. Their huge walled complex across the road was mixed black and white, full of Arnolds and boujee blacks that you couldn't trust, so mostly it was small time, a few cars stopping and carrying the dope out of Culver back into L.A.

"Yo," Li'l Hammer said quickly.

An impressive BMW M3 with blacked out windows approached slowly on the far side of the road. Dudes in that car wouldn't be doing no *buying*. The lights went out and the car stopped in the driveway to the locked-up fire gate that no one ever used. A skinny white man in a cowboy hat got out. Ducks caught a flash of a strange-looking gun in his waist. A bigger white man got out the other side. They said something to one another and then, astonishingly, they boosted one another over the tall gate.

"Ho' shit."

Territoriality asserted itself instantly. Peckerwoods were invading the Astaire, where they'd lived all their lives.

Ducks scooped up his precious bag and locked it into the trunk of the Z28. They sprinted across Jefferson and scaled the gate easily at the corner.

"Who the rover tonight?"

"Bones."

"He no use." Bones was famous for getting drunk on Night Train and passing out behind the laundry. Ducks got out his gray plastic Glock.

"You take the point, oh yeah," Li'l Hammer said gleefully.

"Miami Vice, fuckers."

Li'l Hammer had his 9mm Browning, and they stiff-armed the guns out in front of them with both hands like TV cops, enjoying the rush it gave them. It took them a couple of minutes to track down the invaders, back in a dark alcove that held the entries to four apartments. The bigger man was working at a window with a little crowbar. The apartment belonged to an older white guy who came and went at all hours, always dressed badly. He kept to himself and nobody knew for sure what he did for a living, but somebody said he was a private eye so they called him Dick Tracy.

"Freeze, motherfucker," Ducks said, and then all of a sudden they were all cattycorner and frozen, eight hard eyes staring at a Glock and a Browning, plus a Chief's snubnose .38, and a nasty little Mac-11 with a 32-shot magazine. The Cowboy with the Mac-11 started to laugh.

"We got us enough firepower here to take out a small country. You must be the stud-horses in this here corral."

"You steppin' up to us?" Ducks was astonished that the cowboys didn't seem frightened.

"Oh, no, gentlemen, absolutely no disrespect is intended. It's entirely our mistake to trespass on your territory."

Ducks couldn't make out the man's tone. There wasn't a trace of fear, even caution.

"Now, none of us want to end up a free lunch for the coyotes, do we? So we'll put our guns down and just walk away. Is that satisfactory?"

Ducks didn't know what to say. It wasn't developing at all the way he'd expected. The Cowboy watched him with what looked like amusement. The bigger man regularly squinched up his eyes, as if someone was sticking him with a needle.

"You, see." The little square assault pistol sagged downward and Ducks watched the Cowboy snick on the safety and eject the long plastic magazine. "We take away the irritant, and the only thing that remains between us is respect."

Li'l Hammer was looking to Ducks for a lead.

"But we are bad, gentlemen, and we know how to get the business over with if we have to." The Cowboy's eyes stayed on Ducks, and the atmosphere was shifting imperceptibly toward the polar.

"Go on, beat it," Ducks said.

The Cowboy slowly grinned, the corners of his thin lips spreading wider and wider as if the scar of his mouth would grow until the whole head split in two. A panic began to seep through Ducks and he wanted to run. For the first time in his short life, the pistol offered no comfort at all.

"I think we'll do that, gentlemen," the Cowboy said, but made no motion to leave.

The tension grew unbearable and Ducks felt his pistol crying out, the trigger flexing and daring him to fire.

"It's Miller time, Godzilla," the Cowboy said finally. He laughed again as he took a fistful of the big man's shirt and led him away. They took a long time leaving.

"I dint *like* that," Li'l Hammer said, when they were gone.

"They wasn't after no VHS," Ducks said, eyeing Dick Tracy's window. "No way, Jose."

THE first big rain of the year had begun during the night and had flushed a woman's body out of the storm drains down in Long Beach, but Jack Liffey didn't know anything about that yet. All he knew was that his alarm had gone off, buzzed all the way through its cycle and finally stopped.

He pawed the night table, but it was the gesture of a younger man, a faint species memory of some solace to be found there. An open pack of cigarettes, a shiny brass .30 caliber cartridge casing filled with cocaine, a bottle of scotch. . . . For a few glorious years, he had reached out first light to lay two fingers into the warm hollow at the back of Kathy's neck.

Now his hand found nothing. The emptiness flooded in before he was ready, like a fresh awareness of a death, and his whole body went rigid with the struggle. Just about everything he cared about was gone, and everything now had to be taken neat. And for the first time in his life he wasn't substituting some new addiction: he had locked away the booze, the drugs, the old Raymond Chandler novels, even his daughter's photograph, if only to prove to himself the mathematical purity of his will.

He tipped himself out of bed in one motion, tugged on yesterday's clothes and stared down at the ashtray, with its lone unused cigarette and pristine matchbook. They were all over the apartment, these little failure kits that he never touched. You made your own luck, but only after you proved to yourself that you had a right to it.

He headed out the front door, then halted at the sight of the darkly wet path between the condominium buildings. Weather, he groused, instead of climate. The downspout gurgled softly into the geraniums, and, like most people in L.A., he ignored the cheap folding umbrella and grabbed a cap as he walked out into the rain.

He tugged on the baseball cap as he emerged from the eaves. The cap said Pasadena Penguins. Every time Dan Margolin asked *How 'bout those Dodgers?* he asked back, *How about the Pasadena Penguins?* to show his general contempt for sports, until Margolin finally had the cap made up by one of his aunts. Margolin thought it was a terrific joke.

The mini-mall with his office was ten minutes away across Ballona Creek and he heard the unusual roar of a lot of water as he approached the channel on foot. He came to a dead stop on the bridge, staring down. Somewhere it had rained heavily in the night because Ballona Creek was fast and deep, only he couldn't see water. He could have walked from side to side on the foam cups, billions of them like angular white froth, as the first rains scoured out the gutters and storm drains of the whole city. Between the cups, like punctuation marks, there were thousands of little red spheres, yellow spheres and fluorescent green spheres, bobbing along toward the sea. Finally he guessed that they were tennis balls. He didn't even know they made colored tennis balls. A lawn chair passed on the flow and then something that looked like a large dead dog.

At the strip mall, Marlena Cruz had just opened her Mailboxes-R-Us and she leant forward aggressively, glaring at the tiny monitor on top of her biggest copy machine.

"Waiting for Jay Leno?" he said.

"If it's not one damn thing it's another. This is my penance for not betting it all on some shiny-haired Basque *pelotista*."

She was heavy, fiftyish, strong as an ox and always complaining about joining the petite bourgeoisie. He liked her looks, but she'd have been really stunning in a gypsy way if she'd lost about fifty of the pounds.

"Never bet on Basques," he said. "Never bet on little guys with big grudges."

"Advice is not your specialty, Jack. Not since you went and buy a condo at the top of the market in 1989 and lose all your down."

His mailbox was full. It was mostly junk, offers from CPAs to do bookkeeping for his business, and just about anyone familiar with the placeholding function of the zero could do that. Marlena's mailboxes were more expensive than the post office's, but she provided other services like passing on messages and holding his unregistered .32 Dreyse German submariners' pistol, his cold piece that he didn't want anybody nosy to find in his office upstairs.

He went out to buy a paper from the machine. The *Times'* headline yelled at him inscrutably, *Ter Braak May Head Opera.* What could you do with a newspaper that didn't even know the name of its own city? Nobody but tourists and ex-mayors called L.A. *Los Angeles.*

Marlena leaned out the door. "You used to be a scientist," she said. "Can you make this thing work?"

"It's not what I'm good at."

She preened a bit. "Maybe you could come back late tonight, after I close, and we could find something you're good at."

He smiled. He probably wasn't much good at that any more, either, or at being a father, or at being the kind of friend who gets people through a bad night. If he was good at anything any more, it was just at finding missing kids. Maybe it was enough. He'd discovered his art by accident, and it had saved his bacon when his electronics job became one of the half million in the city to evaporate at the end of the go-go 1980s, just about the same time his marriage did the same.

Just before he ducked into the Coffee Bean, a black BMW pulled out of the mini-mall lot and accelerated away. He noticed it because it was a special order Motorsport model with blacked windows and all the gewgaws. He didn't have enough energy yet to resent the owner.

"The usual," he said.

Dan Margolin looked up from the sports page, his gray pony tail bobbing. "Morning, Lif. Which usual is that? Lox on a bagel?"

"You do and I'll tear your kidneys out and eat them."

Margolin said something else, but he was already behind the paper, reading that L.A. might get some goofy-looking Dutchman named Ter Braak to head a new opera society that the *Times'* owners' wives had been demanding for a year or two. As a phenomenon, opera had about the same interest for him as tooth decay.

Margolin brought his Americanized espresso, strong enough to leave a satisfying sludge in the cup. "How 'bout those Raiders?"

"Is this football season?"

"All winter."

"Is it winter? My wife always said she hated a place where the leaves stayed the same and the air changed colors."

"Rain means winter, Lif. At least in L.A." The toaster popped and Dan Margolin hurried off.

Margolin had been a Marine up in I Corps near Quang Tri. Liffey didn't see how anyone who had been around a war had any time for professional sports—all that noise and spurious loyalty, to no purpose. Of course, his own war had been mostly locked up inside an air-conditioned trailer in Thailand watching a scope and monitoring headphones to see where B-52s were going, the middle-class war.

"Hey, I almost forgot. You got a visitor. She was real insistent. I wouldn't be surprised she's still sitting on your stoop up there."

"Stoop?"

"I think she's right off the boat from Mexico. She didn't speak much English."

Jack Liffey folded the paper over, drank enough coffee so he could see the sludge, and stepped out the door. Craning his neck in the rain, he could see the landing that ran past the upstairs doors. No one was sitting on his non-existent stoop, but he could see that his office door was standing ajar and a chill took his spine. He should probably have sent the cops, but he was stubborn that way.

Jack Liffey ducked into Mailboxes-R-Us. "I need the toy."

"You don't look so good."

"I don't need a lecture."

She went to her storeroom and took down a box that said Red Pencils, then gave him the ugly little .32.

"You be careful, *querido*."

"If I'm not back in half an hour, send for the cavalry."

There was a terrible stillness on the landing, an eerie sense of entering a dream world where luck would end up mattering a whole lot more than any skills he had. He approached the window with his hand on the comforting gun in his pocket. All he could see inside was the little waiting space with its two steel chairs and magazines and the partition with its poster of the Alps from a previous tenant. It all looked okay.

The door had been kicked open, the cheap aluminum frame torn jagged by the deadbolt tongue, and it stood open about a foot. The inner office door was open too, but that was never locked. He sidled in and kept moving slowly toward the inner door.

He took out the .32, his mind not working quite right, and he fought himself into focus. There was enough light through the venetian blinds in back to see quickly that no one was there. It was amazing how fast the fear went away, he thought, as he surveyed the wreckage. It looked more like it had been done to make a point than to search.

"Aw, shit," he said. The goldfish his daughter had given him, last visitation, was dead in a damp patch on the floor. He went back down and got his toast and sat.

For over a year now he had been trying to live in the
present, without much in the way of hopes or dreams,
trying to ignore not only his own sour past, but all the
gratuitous rot and corruption that built up in the city
around him. There was one problem with living too
much in the present, though. When you did get incoming, it tended to be in really big calibers.

"Call the cops for me, Dan."

2

THE SPACE YOU INHABIT

THE BLACK COP HAD BEEN A LOT FRIENDLIER THAN THE white one, but he had gone quiet a while back, poking at the rubble on the floor. His name tag said Black, but Jack Liffey decided it was not something he wanted to be witty about. He had seen them both around town, but hadn't ever run into them.

''You got a gun in here, big guy?'' the belligerent white cop asked.

''In that blue book.'' He'd hollowed out an *Oxford Companion to English Literature* and set it with some other books on the theory that no one in his right mind would ever pick it up.

The cop frowned as he took out the big gray .45 as if he'd finally found the real problem here.

''I assume you got a permit.''

''Nobody's got a permit. It's registered.'' A gazillion detective novels to the contrary, L.A. County did not issue permits to carry concealed weapons.

''Let's see it.''

Jack Liffey nodded at the litter on the floor where all his files had been turned out. ''Help yourself.''

The cop ignored him and turned the pistol over in his

hand like an interesting rodent. "What is it?"

Liffey toyed with saying *It's a gun*, but thought he'd better not. "It's a Ballester-Molina, an Argentine copy of the army issue. I thought I was getting a good deal until I found out none of the parts are interchangeable except the magazines."

The cop looked up at him thoughtfully. The blue name tag said Quinn. "You get a lot of raw deals, do you?"

"Just my share."

"Too bad about the goldfish," the black cop said.

It sounded like he meant it, but he'd be damned if he'd acknowledge it the way the white cop was turning out.

"You working on any interesting 'cases'?" The white cop gave the word a nasty twist.

"I'm not a detective. I just find missing kids."

"You have to shoot a lot of them?"

"Only if they cry," he said.

The white cop glared, but let it go finally.

"Probably some drug-head after your petty cash," Black said.

"Sure."

Quinn dropped the pistol, a bit too hard on the desk so it probably scarred the wood. "Oh, oops there."

"You might want to wipe off your prints," Liffey said. You couldn't let things go indefinitely and end up living with yourself. "You never know where that'll end up."

"You looking for trouble from me?"

Jack Liffey's vision went red. "I'm fifty-two years old, cocksucker," he said very softly and slowly, "and I know more about trouble than you ever will."

They glared at one another until the black cop took his partner's arm and pressed him slowly away. He balled up the multi-part form he'd been writing on and tossed it in the trash. "We'll just skip the burglary report, I think."

"The fuck you will. I need it for the insurance."

"Try the Santa Monica cops," Quinn said. "They're real *polite*."

When they were gone he stared at the door for a long time with his heart racing. In Basic, he'd watched three tough black kids on the long slide downhill go for a timid white boy. Liffey knew if he'd helped, they'd just have got him later, and he'd watched the boy's eyes going sleepier and sleepier with fear.

"You our buddy, Milken, be a buddy and loan us fifty."

"I can't afford it."

"Oh, he can't *afford* it. You a racist motherfucker, you know that? You apologize for being a racist motherfucker."

"Sure, man, I'm sorry."

"*Sure man*. Don't *Sure man* me, racist motherfucker."

The humiliation had gone on and on. Liffey had seen that none of them would ever recover from the things that had made them. He had waited across the barracks, one hand on a scarred baseball bat by his bed. If they'd come his way, he was determined to take down at least one of them. In the end, you only had the space you inhabited, and you couldn't let anyone take that away or it was gone forever.

He looked around the dumped manila folders of old records and began kicking it into piles. So he couldn't claim insurance for the door or anything else that was busted. Another small step in the long decline of expectations of his life.

He froze when he saw the old Xeroxed poster under

his foot. Janelle van der Merwe. A young blond girl, skinny, smiling obligingly, helpless looking. Coming home the long shaky way from Nam in 1970, he'd made friends with some locals in a bar in South Africa and stayed with them for a few weeks and one of them named Gysbert had grown up and married and had kids and then had found Liffey's name somehow two decades later and written to beg him to find his daughter who had gone AWOL from her exchange high school in Ohio, last known postcard from Hollywood. Even now, the stringy blond girl in the photograph didn't look much like what he remembered of Gysbert.

Liffey had made up a lot of copies of the photo, mostly just to say that he'd tried. He informed the police, tacked up posters, and spent an evening on the Strip talking to teenage girls wearing tiny bandeaux where breasts might be some day. He'd amazed himself by finding her inside of a week out in Canyon Country. She'd been a virtual prisoner of a megalomaniac Fundamentalist preacher who enticed runaways off the Strip with a lot of cult mumbo-jumbo and put them to work as unpaid labor sewing fancy bright-colored leather jackets that they sold to the boutiques back down on the Strip, a modern version of the old slave-to-rum-to-slave trade. He'd hired a real private eye to help him break in and snatch the girl and he'd found out that he, Liffey, was tougher and more alert than the rummy ex-cop and did most of it himself.

Liffey had got a whiff of the thrill of the hunt, and five years later that skill had been his tenuous lifeline out of the collapse of his life.

He was startled by a hesitant knock on the open outside door. An old Latina in a shawl with a crumpled letter in her hand watched him with Indian eyes and for some reason he knew immediately she was straight up from Mexico and had a hard luck story. His heart sank because he didn't do very well finding kids on the east side. He'd only succeeded once, and now he usually referred missing Latinos to Art Castro, who'd helped him out that time.

"Mr. Leefee? You speak Spanish, please?" She was damp through.

"*Momentito*."

He went past her, on his way to get Marlena and bring her up and then realized he had nowhere to bring her. He turned back. "*Vamanos, senora*, please. Come this way."

They waited in the front of the shop like petitioners while Marlena Cruz sent a fax for an old man in suspenders and white shoes.

"Can you close up and meet us in the Bean?"

She cocked her head dubiously, then looked at the woman and assented with a small flick of her eyebrows. "Your place up there bad?"

"It'll do."

He led the woman into the coffee shop, stabbing a finger at Dan Margolin with his hand held high. He wasn't quite sure himself what the motion meant, perhaps just an odd gesture to put Margolin off balance and insist he treat this occasion with seriousness.

"Three coffees, Dan." To the woman, "*Quiere usted* coffee? Please."

"Thank you very, sir."

They sat at the window. He was uneasy, as he always was when he couldn't communicate. It was like being disarmed. Restlessly, he got up and went to the counter. "This the woman who came earlier?" he said softly.

"Yeah, that's her. What was all the cops up there?"

"Somebody busted into my place. Must have thought I had some cash."

"How'd you like Quinn?"

"A sweetheart. You know him?"

"He's a horse's ass. Last year, I had a panhandler in here bugging people. When he wouldn't leave, I called the cops and they sent *him*. He started roughing up the poor guy and when I objected, the son-of-a-bitch drew down on me. In my own cafe."

It made Liffey feel good to hear that someone else had had a run-in with Quinn, like hearing that other people, too, had the disease with the funny name that they just found on your blood test. They got back to the table just as Marlena arrived and Margolin made himself scarce.

"Thanks," he said. "You're a princess."

She talked to the woman in Spanish and it went on for a long time with various expressions crossing their faces, like cloud shadows on a plain. He was revising his opinion of her as he watched her speak in her own language. What he had taken as peasant timidity was probably only unfamiliarity with English. She seemed more astute in Spanish, almost self-assured. There was also something a little neurotic in her eyes from time to time, and peons were never allowed to be neurotic. He guessed she was a schoolteacher in a small town.

Finally, Marlena looked at him quizzically. "She wants to know if the mission for Senora Beltran involved sending her away from town."

He stared blankly for a moment. "Mission to Neptune, you mean. Are you sure you're translating right? What is *this* woman's name?"

Marlena asked her.

"Maria Elena Schuler. *Habito en Hermosillo.*"

"Schuler?" he said.

"Goodness, Jack. We know Americans named Azizian and Vukovsky."

"And Chan. Fair enough. Hang on, I do know a Senora Beltran." He racked his brain. "Consuela Beltran. It was her son I found a couple years ago. He'd run away looking for his dad, turned up in Modesto." He could see the woman's face light up. A flock of very loud motorcyles passed outside and the glass window vibrated in pain. On the high back seat of one of the Harleys a woman in a mini-skirt flailed at the driver with her fists, as if she were being kidnaped in a bad biker movie, and he puzzled over the image. He sipped at the coffee, but it was ordinary coffee and terrible.

"Let's do this in order. Is Senora Beltran missing?" The two women talked for a while.

"She's been missing for more than a week. Maria Elena is her mother and they exchange letters every week. The last letter, dated two weeks ago, said that Senora Beltran was coming to see you to get you to help her with a problem."

"Tell her she never showed up. And find out more."

While they talked, his eye involuntarily followed a young couple who had come in and taken a table against the wall. The girl was astonishingly beautiful with big hair, like some starlet who had wandered down Overland from Sony Columbia, the studio up the road that had been MGM before a corporate pirate had stripped and dismembered it. The boy with her was lame and had a bad scar on his cheek. It was the kind of lack of parity that made you suspicious, looking for the adjustments.

"The boy is only thirteen and Senora Beltran made no arrangements for anyone to look after him so she is afraid something bad happened. She didn't come back from her job last Tuesday."

"The job is?"

The boy with the scar was hissing something, and the girl, who thought she couldn't be heard, said quite dis-

tinctly, "My pussy is not for you, so get that straight."
There was a terrible spoiled whicker in her voice and
right away he saw one of the adjustments.

"She was secretary for the Cahuenga Neighborhood
Organization. I know them. They elected a slate of Chi-
canos last year and threw out the old Anglo fuddy-
duddys that had ran the town forever."

"News first, editorials later," he said.

Marlena gave a feral grin that he hadn't seen very
often. "Everybody gets the translator they deserve. You
should learn the first language of the town you live in."

"I'm too old and too dumb. Have the cops been no-
tified?"

He could see her shake her head, and he pushed on
to short-circuit the roundabout process. "Is the ex-
husband in the picture, or anyone else living in?"

There was no one living in, the boy was with an aunt,
and the house was undisturbed, not even a suitcase missing. Senora Schuler had no clear idea what the problem
was that her daughter was supposed to be bringing to
Liffey, but it had something to do with unspecified
threats. The daughter respected Liffey because he had
been *simpatico* and he had found the boy Tony pretty
quickly.

"I seem to remember *simpatico* is one of those trou-
blesome words that doesn't mean quite what you think
it does."

"It's something like *decent*."

"I remember Senora Beltran and I'd like to help her
if I could. She was real *simpatico*. But Senora Schuler
would be better off hiring a guy I know named Art Castro."

Marlena explained and the woman shook her head
adamantly.

''She wants you, because her daughter trusted you. And she's got some money.''

''That always helps.'' He considered for a long time. He would be a fish out of water in Cahuenga, though he didn't have a lot on his plate at the moment and a little income never hurt. His eyes swung around as he thought it over, just in time to catch the blonde girl do something strange. She wrenched open her blouse angrily to her companion, like a flasher. Her back was to the room so he couldn't see if she was wearing a bra, but the boy with the scar went goggle-eyed.

''Satisfied?'' the girl blurted. She clutched the blouse tight as she skedaddled with angry red eyes.

''Get all the addresses and names, would you? I'll spend a day or two on it and see if it looks like I can do any good.''

''Thank you very, Mr. Leefee,'' she said when it was explained. She unfolded a small piece of paper and handed it to him. *Call Liffey. Threats. Slow Growth.*

''I want you to buy me a drink for this,'' Marlena Cruz said, and he could see that she meant it.

HE stared mournfully at the plastic card for a long time before inserting it into the Culver Bank ATM. This was the account the court didn't know about, the one he'd sworn to himself was for Maeve's college, and every month the bottom line got smaller. The money was almost half gone now.

He'd replace what he drew down when someone paid him big, when he got a job, when his ship came in. It was like gambling, and once you started you couldn't stop. All he was doing was paying the rent and buying gas. That didn't make it okay, but it was just another sidestep in the gradual development of portable ethics.

3

A TOXIC HORMONE SPILL

"It's Norman French, believe it or not. There used
to be an E on the end, but somebody a few generations
back dropped it. I've got cousins still spelled with the
E.''

Her name was Eleanor Ong and since he hadn't seen
a wedding ring, he'd said she didn't look like an Ong.
Actually she looked a bit like a whippet, skinny and
nervous and fast, with freckles and a lot of limp dark
hair with red and gray highlights. She had an unruly
energy about her that he found attractive.

''It's only been my name again for two years and
sometimes I forget to respond. I was Sister Mary Rose
for fifteen years.''

He let that roll past. They sat in a decaying storefront
that had been built onto the front of a huge old frame
house on Slauson that was now the Catholic Liberation
house in southeast L.A. A big flowery sign over a water
cooler said: *Close all the factories of crime—jails and
prisons!*

''That's her desk. We gave them office space when
we worked together on the city council election last year.
She's been helpful to us, too. They can get offset print-

ing on the cheap.'' It was a battered old oak post office desk, like all the others in the big room, including the one where Eleanor Ong sat with one foot on the open bottom drawer. She wore one of those long rayon gypsy skirts and flat leather sandals that strapped around her hairy ankles and reminded him of an aging graduate student.

''Who would her boss be? I'd like to get permission to look through the desk.''

She screwed up her face. It was the first time he'd seen her slow down. ''I guess the whole committee. She's the only paid staff, though they've got a chairperson. I'll call for you and see what I can do. I hope you don't mind if I smoke.''

''What if I did?''

''You could always sit in the no-smoking section.''

She pointed to the street. A young man in a Pendleton shirt came out of a back room while she was lighting up. He whispered to her, showing a handful of papers. All the Catholic Liberation kids he'd ever met were earnest and intense and very clean. They still believed deeply in good and evil, so that even being witty about it was seen as a bit of a sin.

''If he goes near the shelter again, have them call the police.''

For some time, a banging noise outside had been working at his attention. The rain had stopped and two squat men were chopping sheet metal pieces off an old Ford Galaxie from the 1960s that was parked in front of a boarded-up trophy manufacturer. The operation seemed pointless.

''Make sure they know we don't let husbands carry on like that. And send them a copy of the restraining order, in case somebody needs to see it.''

The young man nodded portentously and went back inside.

"It'll probably take me a while to get in touch with enough members of the committee. You could give me a ring or come back this afternoon. Other than that, I can't really give you permission to go through her things, even with her mother's okay."

"That's fine. You could tell me more about Mrs. Beltran. Anything you know."

"Where'd you go to high school?" she asked out of the blue.

"It wasn't a Catholic school. San Pedro."

"I knew a guy, the name was something like Liffey. I think what reminds me's not the name, it's that alert air you've got, you know, taciturn but fierce, polite to women and small children but hell on wheels when you run into other raptors."

"You've got an edge on you yourself."

"You try being a virgin for seventeen years. That'll give you an edge that salutes."

She stared straight at him, as if daring him to take it as flirtation. He laughed instead. "About Mrs. Beltran."

She banged the cigarette on a glass saucer. "She should be a real success story. She has a mind like . . . I don't know. Maybe she's a genius, maybe just shrewd. If she'd been born a man she'd be teaching in some college as the star Latino scholar or, if she'd lost her ethics somewhere along the way, she'd be arbitraging GM.

"Her husband couldn't handle it. She had spirit, and she wouldn't shut up when she knew she was right. After he took off, she went to school and got a B.A. at City in History. Her specialty was 20th century California; we used to talk about Carey McWilliams. She's working on her doctorate at L.A. State in sociology."

He was beginning to feel very uncomfortable about himself. He'd met Consuela Beltran twice and hadn't seen very much of that. He'd seen a small brown overweight woman, a bit nervous, who looked a lot like a million other Latinas with a dozen kids at home. Articulate and quick, but not to take special note. How the hell did you avoid that snap stupid racism? And still get on with living? Your liberal grandmother could pretend she wasn't worried when she ran into a half dozen young blacks in bandannas on a dark street. They might all be Rhodes scholars, but she'd be insane to count on it.

"She can see right through most pretense. It's what makes her good in the neighborhood organization. She can sort out the hidden agendas and who needs a few extra strokes of praise and who needs to feel in charge and all that."

"Were there fights in the organization?"

"Like any living organization. There were plenty of mixed motives to go around. Some people have to dominate. Some people just like to hear themselves talk. Putting up with that malarkey is the curse of democracy. Have you ever been in a grass-roots organization?"

"Does the Army count?"

She laughed. "Not unless your platoon voted on what you did next."

"That's a thought." He liked the laugh and he wondered how he would handle long hairy legs. He'd never been with a woman who didn't shave.

"She was up against a group that called itself Cahuenga Slow Growth. Basically they were dead white males, the businessmen who'd run the town for generations. Backed up by a lot of retired Anglo working people who haven't fled to Orange County. Slow Growth really meant Enforce the Zoning so we don't have all these Mexicans and Central Americans doubling up in our houses and crowding us out.

"Nobody likes seeing two or three poor families crammed into a small house, but until this society provides something better for immigrants we can't just throw them out on the street. Can you imagine the struggle, raising a family on minimum wage plus a few extra bucks selling oranges on the on-ramp? You don't rent a big condo in Brentwood on that. Besides, the Slow Growth people were all the children of Okies who doubled up in the houses here in the thirties, they just don't remember."

"You sound like you might have been one of them once."

She shook her head. "I grew up in Inglewood. Of course, before it was black. I come from probably three generations of middle-class lawyers."

"How could an Anglo group hope to win here?"

"Their literature was full of code words like *blight* and *unsightly*. It didn't say Beaners once."

"That's not enough."

"No, it's not enough." She slowed down again, and made a face as if she was about to have family secrets dragged out of her. "You'll find a fair number of established Mexican-Americans who don't like the newer undocumented, too. It's an attitude that's changing, but it's there. You know, last one on the ark shut the door."

"Was the campaign bitter?"

"When isn't a threat to someone's power? It didn't seem to get personalized, because there was no one spokesperson for the Neighborhooders."

He unfolded the note Senora Schuler had given him and showed it to her. *Call Liffey. Threats. Slow growth.*

"Is that her handwriting?"

She turned the yellow Post-it over a few times,

walked quickly to the desk she'd identified as Consuela Beltran's and picked up a pad of yellow Post-its. They were the same size but of course that didn't prove anything.

"Can I see it?" he asked.

She brought it back and set the blank pad in front of him. He took a pencil out of a marmalade jar on her desk, whittled it down with his Swiss Army knife until he could break out a half inch of lead and then ran the flat of the lead lightly over the pad. The faint impression might have been the same as the note, but that didn't prove much either.

"You really are a detective."

"I saw it in Dick Tracy."

"It doesn't make any sense. The election's been over almost a year, and 'threats' just isn't their style. Did she call you?"

"Not that I know of, but my machine's been known to go out."

"It's very strange."

The banging outside changed pitch. They seemed to have started in on the car with a bigger hammer. A timer went off deep in the house.

"I've got to go downtown to our soup kitchen now, my turn to serve, but give me a ring this afternoon."

"Do you mind if I ask you why you dropped out?"

"Dropped out?"

"Secularized? However it's put."

"I'm not sure we know each other well enough."

"That could be arranged."

She laughed. "I was pregnant by a priest. He stayed a priest, the jerk, got himself transferred to Albuquerque. There's a place they send nuns, but I wasn't having any. Call me later about the desk."

"My pleasure."

Outside the humidity hit him. L.A. was so rarely humid that it was always a shock. The two car-wreckers seemed to be reducing the sheet metal of the Ford to breadboard-sized pieces. He noticed that Slauson crossed the L.A. River just down a long block and he walked that way out of curiosity, wondering if it was filled with foam cups, too. He passed a fairly new mini-mall with Mi Playa Tortas y Mariscos, a Fotografia and the inevitable donut shop. Further on was a nurses' and bus drivers' uniform supply and a dead movie house, with a lobby card for *Coal Miner's Daughter*. All the buildings had indecipherable graffiti in that angular city scrawl.

The water ran high and fast between concrete banks, foaming on the bridge supports. It was about three times wider than Ballona Creek. There were no cups, no flotsam at all, perhaps it had been scoured into the bay already. Bright floats on ropes dangled from the bridge, to grab onto if you fell in. Every year like clockwork during high water a few people lost their footing and were chased downstream from bridge to bridge by fire-trucks and TV crews. Some managed to grab ropes they were thrown and some drowned.

The sound of the water was a little too fast to be soothing, but he still liked watching the racing dark surface. He wondered why people always found solace in moving water. You could just as easily see a cosmic indifference, a process of wear and erosion that would go on without you and go on until everything on earth was worn away.

A flotilla of schoolkids came toward him across the bridge, all loud bantering and fists against shoulders. Two or three danced at the periphery with a mean edge. Something had happened since his day. It was as if the country had gone through a toxic hormone spill and even the six-year-olds had to train up to spear lions. This group was black, brown and white in almost equal numbers, all wearing some flash of green, a bandanna or a shirt. He'd thought kids never ganged up across race, but here was the evidence. That was something to be said for Cahuenga.

They were almost past when a trailing white kid turned back.

"Hey, man, watcha lookin' at?"

"Just thought I'd look at the river."

Two blacks came back to help out.

"That's some strange shit, man. Look at the river? What for?"

"I don't know," Jack Liffey said, still feeling amiable, though he could sense the trouble brewing. "Do you always know why you do things?"

"Are you saying I'm stupid? You're a pussy."

The two black kids fanned out to block him against the concrete railing. He guessed they were about fourteen or fifteen, but one of them was taller than he was. The rest of the gang hung out at the end of the bridge, watching casually.

"Man, you're stealing our Jesus."

"Yeah, motherfucker, you're dissing our Jesus."

There was nothing that could be said to that so he just stared neutrally back, waiting to see what move they'd make.

"Gimme your wallet," the white kid said.

The black kid on his right tugged a silk shirt out of his waistband to show the handle of a cheap 9mm Star.

"Don't fuck with us, man."

"No trouble."

He took out his city wallet with his left hand and handed it over. The white kid snatched it and they all ran.

"Have a nice day," he called. The Dreyse was in his

coat pocket, but it wasn't worth getting someone hurt. Besides, his real wallet was still in his right rear pocket. The city wallet held two outdated credit cards, some random business cards from insurance agents, the photo of Jim Garner that had come with the cheap wallet, and a ten-dollar bill so a mugger wouldn't get too angry.

He wondered if it was something to do with meeting Eleanor Ong that had kept him feeling good-humored through it all.

4

PEELING THE ONION

HE WAS STANDING AND WAVING ONE ARM, COMPLAINING about twinges in the shoulder, nitrogen bubbles from a deep dive. Jack Liffey took the weight belt from him and tossed it into the cracked sea chest. They were rocking softly on a ratty old shrimper tied up at the end of Fish Harbor in San Pedro. The sky was overcast and dark in the afternoon.

Only Mike Lewis would go scuba diving in the lull of a rainstorm, he thought. He'd probably wedged it in between his classes in urban theory, whatever that was, and a hell-bent dash in his old Toyota to some TV interview. Somewhere in there he wrote books on L.A. social history.

"Before you get the bends, have some of this."

Jack Liffey handed him the fifth of unblended scotch. He hadn't touched it himself, and wouldn't, but a bottle was *de rigueur* on a visit to Lewis. He was a little feisty restless guy, a former SDS leader who'd been black-balled from the big schools for years so he'd taught part-time in little art colleges. Then he wrote a probing social history of L.A., about who'd gored whose ox, that became so hot the *Times* and the talk shows couldn't get enough of him.

"The only time I can catch up with you is when you're diving. All I've got to do is look for air bubbles."

"Dig out a sweatshirt, will you?"

Toni Mardesich, the wiry old man who owned the boat, did something skillful looking and nautical with a heavy rope and stepped ashore. "Last one off button the flaps."

"Thanks for the ride, Toni."

"Any time, Mikie."

Fish Harbor was sad. The big Japanese tuna boats with their ten-mile draglines had killed off the industry, and the American boats with their third-generation Italian and Yugoslav crews rarely went out any more. He remembered as a kid the bustle of the wharf, with old men repairing nets and young men hurrying back and forth, and the fabulous pageant of Fisherman's Fiesta every year, decorated boats parading up and down the channel to be blessed by some bishop, all of which was long gone. The boats sat and decayed. Taking Mike out was probably just something to do for a guy who was bored and broke. Mike Lewis seemed to know everybody.

He looked even smaller in the huge dark sweatshirt. They sat and stared out over the gray channel toward the dead tuna packing plant on Terminal Island, a single seagull swooping and crying over the water. It was a view that for some reason had no sense of intimacy at all. It was the stillest he'd ever seen Lewis.

"I remember Consuela Beltran," Mike Lewis said. "I met her when I was writing the piece on the Cahuenga election. A really strong woman with big brown eyes who always wanted to talk about post-structuralism."

"Funny, she never asked me about it."

There was a scuffling on the wharf and they both looked over at a mountain of rotted net and oblong floats where some kids were playing king of the hill, apparently in two teams, skins and shirts. Skins were winning, rougher than Jack Liffey remembered similar games on Averill Park's big hill. They looked like they were maybe twelve or thirteen.

"Tell me about the elections."

"The Latinos won all three contested seats and it's now three to two on the council. It's the first city council in the county with a Latino majority. Latinos are so disaffected only about thirty percent of them vote. And of course a lot are still Mexican citizens."

"What's the significance of *la gente* winning?"

"Who said it was *la gente* who won?"

"Catholic Liberation's on their side. They can't be all bad."

Lewis beckoned for another hit of scotch. "That's good stuff, but I prefer Irish." He was married to a fast-talking Irishwoman he'd met in a decade of self-imposed exile, and he still affected a lot of Irish mannerisms like buying rounds in a bar and carrying wooden matches. "Nothing's all bad. But you've got to peel the onion and see what's underneath. You read my piece right after the election."

Liffey grimaced. "I think I must have missed it."

Lewis tutted once. "That ex-nun with the long legs would like to think she was part of a crusade against geriatric Anglo capitalists, but the Cahuenga Neighborhood Organization got a lot of their war chest from slumlords, Anglo, Latino and Korean. Two families a house, five, ten—the more the better. It doesn't make it all crooked. It's just another fact."

"An unpleasant fact to some."

He shrugged. "Facts are just facts. Activists like Jorge Gallegos felt they were using the slumlords. They took the money and used it to get some Latinos in office. Of course, one of the candidates was a developer and the others were pals of realtors, even if they had vowels on the ends of their names."

There was a sharp scream on the net mountain. It looked like a shirt had fallen backward and hit his head, with his allies clustered around. The skins looked down sheepishly. Jack Liffey wondered if it was cynical or just realistic to call war the human condition. Peace was the aberration. War kept reasserting itself, and he was having trouble formulating any philosophy that made it acceptable.

He stirred as if to go intervene, but Lewis touched his arm. "You don't know enough about it."

"I'm not bad with kids."

The hand tightened on his bicep. "Don't be a fucking liberal."

The kid-war seemed to be simmering down, and Liffey tilted back his head and let the sea air cool the underside of his chin.

"We probably won't know who was using whom in Cahuenga until we see their votes a year from now. More social services, or just more slums."

"My dad used to have a saying for a situation like that," Liffey said. "Whether the vase hits the hammer or the hammer hits the vase, it's the vase that breaks."

Lewis raised his eyebrows. "Meaning, it's the big dogs that eat. True. I have a sense there's even more layers to the onion. I just don't have time to look into it."

They both ducked when they heard the first shot. It was followed by a half dozen more, small and shrill like a .22, and when Liffey finally managed a peek over the gunwale he saw a group of shirts running, carrying one of their number spread-eagled between them. The skins weren't to be seen.

"Jesus, kids," Liffey said. "What do your post-structuralist friends say about twelve-year-olds with guns?"

"You wouldn't fret so much if you had a sufficiently inclusive embrace of the human experience."

Liffey looked around and frowned at him until Lewis broke into a grin. " 'I am large, I contain multitudes. I am not the poet of goodness only, I do not decline to be the poet of wickedness also.' I like things a little ragged."

"Don't be an asshole."

THE rain held off and after trying a pay phone that had had its armored cable sawed half through and one with the quarter slot impossibly jammed with burnt matches, he finally found a working model outside a bar on Pacific just up from Fish Harbor. There was some sort of commotion at the other end.

"Ms. Ong, please."

"Just a sec."

The instant she came on he could hear that she was crying.

"This is Jack Liffey. Is something wrong?"

"Oh, God. Mr. Liffey. You'd better come over here. She's dead. Consuela's dead."

"What happened?"

"She drowned in the L.A. River. It's *horrible*."

She seemed to have lost most of her cocky fortitude, and he felt a chill go through him. "I'll be there."

THE warm damp made his steering wheel feel sticky, as if it had been shellacked. He drove straight up the

Harbor Freeway and east out Gage, past all the abandoned plants and past what was almost a shanty town with rows of tiny peeling shacks that supported cardboard and tin add-ons in between. The flat light from the overcast sky was merciless, allowing no shadows or hidden corners. He hadn't been this way in years and it surprised him L.A. had a slum that rivaled South Africa. She was waiting for him in front of the Liberation house in a fluffy white sweater. Her eyes were red and he had an overwhelming urge to touch her as she got in.

"She was so darn vital."

"Who found her?"

"The police came by. They said she'd been in the water a long time. It's unbelievable. She floated all the way to Long Beach and they found her near the Queen Mary."

Eleanor Ong held her face to wipe her tears surreptitiously. He wondered if she'd known the woman that well or she just cried a lot.

"Did they say anything about wounds or marks?"

"They weren't very forthcoming. They wouldn't be, would they?"

"You never know. Some cops are just people."

"Left here. It's a couple blocks up on the right."

There were a lot of small bungalows from the 1920s done up with stucco and arched entries the way Latinos did, fairly tidy lawns, a few apartment houses. There was no question which house. People were scattered around the neighborhood staring at it as if it was about to stand up and do something entertaining, and two police cars were in front, though not black and whites. Cahuenga P.D. used a fat beige stripe on the side of their white cars, as if they were a rich suburb trying for designer law enforcement. One of the cars left as he approached and he parked almost a block away.

"It's up there," she said.

"I kind of figured that out," he said. Two cars was too much for an accidental drowning, maybe even three if the white Lumina was a police plainwrap. "Have you been here much?"

"A few times. I brought her home once in a while, and I had dinner with them twice. I stayed with Tony once when she had some election work."

"Was there ever any sign of the husband?"

She shrugged. "There's a photo, but if you're asking if I saw any cigar butts in the ashtrays, no."

"No other men?"

"Mr. Liffey, are you investigating her?"

"I'm getting curious. Come on, call me Jack or I'll call you Sister Mary Rose."

She blushed as she got out. He hadn't seen a woman blush in a long time. For all her tough front, she was still a nun.

"Jack. It's such a macho name."

"Jack be nimble," he said with an apologetic smile. "It wasn't my fault."

The house was the front bungalow of a court, eight identical Spanish tile buildings that faced each other across a walking path that ran up from the street. A big brass B was beside the door. The one with the A had a tiny grotto with a statue of the virgin square in the middle of its meager share of grass. Toward the back, about E, a very heavy woman hid herself ineffectually on the stoop behind an open screen door.

"What should I say?" Eleanor Ong said just before they stepped up on the porch toward the open door.

"Whatever they ask. You don't fuck with—screw with cops if you can help it."

"I don't shock that easy, Jack."

"We'll see about that."

They were both startled by his tone, but by then they were half way into the overcrowded living room. Two uniforms, and two shoes, he noted. The shoes were both paunchy and older, probably Cahuenga's only detectives. One was a Latino, and the other had a nice florid Celtic face. Maria Elena Schuler sat on the sofa, red-faced but trying hard not to break down in front of all these foreigners as she spoke softly to a woman her age. Liffey recognized the boy, two years older than when he'd brought him back down from the Central Valley. He sat next to his grandmother, wearing only a white sleeveless T-shirt to show off his homemade tattoo, fierce as a warrior. The barrio warrior recognized Liffey and the boy inside almost nodded. There were several others, neighbors or relatives sitting on all the chairs, or standing behind them.

The Latino cop noticed them in the doorway, and his curiosity quotient shot up. Senora Schuler followed the detective's gaze and recognized the newcomers. She spoke rapidly to her companion and the Latino cop overheard. He detached himself and crossed the room like a tugboat steaming slowly upchannel. Liffey noticed a woven leather holster clipped over his waist, something he'd seen on Mexican plainclothes cops in Baja.

"Hello, Miss Ong." His eyes sought out Jack Liffey, steel gray and very serene eyes. "What's your interest here?" He hadn't actually crossed the border into rudeness, but his passport was ready.

"Mrs. Schuler hired me to try to find her daughter."

"Private detective?"

Liffey shook his head. "No. Usually I just find missing kids. My name is Jack Liffey. I found Tony two years ago, and they remembered me."

"Did you find anything this time?"

"I just started this morning. You should see this."

He handed over the note. He could hear Eleanor Ong breathing nearby and he liked it.

"I'm glad you offered without any prompting. I've heard about the note." His eyes scanned it over and over, as if it might yield up a new meaning eventually.

"I think someone else knows about the note. My office was torn to pieces last night. It might be connected, might not."

"You let us do the detecting, okay?"

"Just offering."

The note went into the plainclothes cop's shirt pocket and the gray eyes found him again.

"How do you like slumming over here?" The tone was still neutral, quizzical, like a man who spent his life prodding everything around himself, absent-mindedly tweaking free nerve ends to see which would squeak.

"You don't know enough about me to say that. I've been cooperative, Lieutenant. . . ."

"Zuniga. It is lieutenant. Lieutenant Nestor Zuniga." His expression broke slightly, and a fist pressed softly into Jack Liffey's shoulder. It was impossible to tell whether the gesture was friendly or prelude to something else. "Don't get rattled so easy, Mr. Liffey. Most of us in Cahuenga don't like the big Mercedeses that come down out of Brentwood every once in a while to see what a barrio looks like. And most of us in the department don't like amateurs prowling around."

Liffey came very near saying something intentionally insulting, like, Maybe all those guys from Brentwood are looking for their TVs. "Do you mind if I ask why you think Senora Beltran was murdered?"

Lieutenant Zuniga's eyes narrowed. "How would you know that, now?"

"Nobody sends homicide detectives to an accidental death. Even in the barrio." Generally anger just made things hard to see and he was trying very hard not to get angry.

"You and me are gonna get along, I can see it. That's my partner over there. His name is Sergeant Blanchard Millan. Why don't you go ask him?" It was almost a dare.

Jack Liffey walked straight across the room to where Sergeant Millan was writing on a small metal clipboard. He wrote fast in stiff childish block letters. Liffey squatted next to the boy.

"Hi, Tony. Remember me?"

"Uh-huh."

"Nice tattoo. Did I ever show you mine?" The boy's right shoulder showed the usual blurry homemade blue tattoo, like a ballpoint note left in the rain. It looked like it said C60L.

"No, Mr. Liffey." He was polite, despite his better instincts. "You got a real tattoo?"

Senora Beltran noticed Liffey now and spoke at him rapidly in Spanish. It seemed impolite to interrupt for a translation. The cop stopped writing and watched, breathing heavily through his mouth. It made him look stupid, but Jack Liffey doubted it. Very few idiots made sergeant.

"I'll show you later."

"Slow down," Sergeant Millan said. "Who's this guy?"

Tony Beltran explained, and annoyance crept into the cop's face.

"Your lieutenant sent me over here to ask why you suspect foul play."

"Oh, did he?" He glanced across the small room, but Lieutenant Zuniga had taken Eleanor Ong out onto the porch and was speaking to her with real intensity, as if reopening a family quarrel. The sun had come out and shone magically through her softly billowing skirt.

"You don't want me to bother Mrs. Schuler with it, do you?"

"There were rope burns on her wrists, but no ropes when we found her."

"How long had she been dead?"

"Ten days, couple weeks. We don't know the cause of death yet, but there were no major wounds."

"Isn't it odd she wasn't found sooner?"

The cop said nothing and Liffey felt a small hand on his shoulder. "Grandma wants you to find out who killed my mother."

"I can't do that, Tony. It's for the police."

"Damn straight, *senor*," the cop said. It was the worst pronunciation of the word *senor* he'd ever heard and must have been intentional.

"Thanks for the information, sergeant. I won't be in your way." He rested a hand on Tony's forearm, felt the stringy muscle. It reminded him of his daughter's arm, which reminded him of innocence, which made him feel bad as it always did. "Show me where you work out."

They went out a side door, where a shed off the side of the house covered a homemade weight bench. The boy had a rusted set of barbells and several cans of concrete with pipe handles. When he was sure no one was looking, he put his arms around the boy and the boy wept inconsolably. They had had most of a day together driving back down 99. He'd taken him to Castle Air Base outside Modesto and talked to him about the B-29 and the Phantom and the other planes, and they'd eaten tacos in a dive in Delano. Then he'd told him about Cesar Chavez, who was barely a recognizable name to the boy. He had liked Tony and thought him far too smart for the tattoo and the gangbanging and all of that, but that was none of his business. Adults almost never changed kids.

"Your mom was a wonderful woman, a very smart woman."

That redoubled the tears, but eventually the boy ran down and they sat side by side on the weight bench. Jack Liffey rolled up his sleeve.

"What does Good Conduct mean, man?"

"It was a Viet Nam thing. It was supposed to keep me out of trouble." He shrugged. "I'm still here, so part of it worked. What's C60L?"

"That's the Cahuenga 60th Street Locos."

"You into the heavy stuff?"

"No, man. We're just taggers, you know? You see our tags on all the buildings along 60 and 61."

"I'll look for them. Do you have a nickname?"

"I'm T-Bell."

"Okay, T-Bell. Have your grandmother call me in a few days, when the cops are all gone."

"Are you gonna help us?"

"It may not be necessary."

Just then one of the men leaned out the door and hissed for Tony. "*Vamos*, Tonito."

5

YOU'RE FUCKED WE'RE YOUR FUTURE

"**WOULD YOU MIND DRIVING ME UP TO PICO RIVERA? THE**
Northrup plant." The wind plastered her skirt against
slim legs, and he would have driven her to the moon,
or tried. He leaned across to open the door.

"I take it you're not looking for a job as a machin-
ist."

It was a thin smile. "We picket every Friday. That's
where they make the Stealth bomber. Do you know how
much they could have done for this country with the
money they're wasting—even the last few planes—now
that they know there's no point making them at all?"

"Two hospitals in every garage," he said. He headed
south for Florence instead of going back to Gage. It was
good to give this side of town the once-over.

She wasn't sure how to take him. "You probably
don't approve. You were in Viet Nam, weren't you?"

A red light caught him in front of a labor mosca and
he grimaced. Scores of squat brown Central Americans
were swarming a stake truck, shouting and waving and
begging for work, and two mean-looking gringos in the
truck bed shouted back at them and pushed them away
from the sides. Three others tried to flag down a pickup

heading out of the do-it-yourself store. It would refute something basic in you, he thought, to have to stand there day after day selling yourself like that. He was thankful when the light changed, though he had to cram on the brake to miss a city bus coming through late.

"*Shit*. Sorry." It took him a moment to control the flash of rage. Why did he have this terrible temper? "The point isn't really the cost, is it? I don't like war much more than the next guy, if it can be helped. I just don't see the point of empty gestures."

"What do you mean?" She wriggled around to take off the angora sweater and reveal a strange ruffled blouse. He hadn't seen a sweater like that since the days of poodle skirts. He recalled the little clip chains girls wore in high school to hold the sweater over their shoulders like a cape.

"I can see marching somewhere to seize a building, or sitting down in front of a train, *doing* something. I can even see it when there's a chance of swinging public opinion, like kids burning their draft cards in 1964. I can't see going week after week when nothing happens."

"You don't believe in moral witness, then?"

He didn't really want to argue. There was never any point arguing about ideas. "I'm sure you're not hurting anybody. It's just not for me. Tell me about Lieutenant Zuniga. You guys looked like old friends."

She watched him a moment before shifting her conversational gears, as if deciding whether she wanted to follow him down his path. "We had a run-in over the gravedigger's strike three years ago. When the contract came up, the new cardinal got it in his head to bust the union, or at least he stonewalled like that's what he was doing. He brought in strikebreakers and insisted on a wage cut. It's not like the diocese is broke, but you can always get manual labor cheaper if you haven't got a conscience. Look at that labor market we just saw. Do you know what they pay day labor?''

"Fifty a day."

"And some of the contractors cheat them on that.'' He could see there were a lot of things that worked her up.

"Lieutenant Zuniga," he said gently.

"We had mass picketing at Saint Teresa's and they got an injunction against it. The lieutenant enforced the injunction.''

"How?"

"He was clever. He arrested me, and no matter how many times I said it was okay, the men were too gallant to let me stay in jail. They stopped the sitdown. I'm still ashamed that my presence may have hurt the strike.''

"Outside of being cunning, is he honest?"

"I really don't think I would have any way of knowing. You know, I don't even think it would help me to know. At Catholic Liberation we try to deal with the world on the up and up. You approach people in a straightforward way and they usually have to respond that way, too. Even if they don't, you've behaved correctly.''

"It's a nice idea but I kind of prefer getting results, I think," he said. "Philosophically speaking, and as a systematic canon. Here's your friends.''

There were eight of them marching a small loop outside the main gate, older women, a few twenty-something men. *Make War no More. Stealth Steals from the Poor. B-2 Be Sorry.* He realized suddenly that the plant was built on the site where the old Ford factory had been. Little by little L.A. had lost all its auto plants, and all its steel, rubber and aluminum. Only the aircraft industry was left and he knew this plant was slated to go, too, in a couple of years.

He stopped in a bus zone, just near enough to hear the picketers singing a hymn, and he could see he had upset her a bit. "I'm sorry if I annoyed you. Something is riding me."

"It's okay. I don't have to limit myself to chatting with the converted."

"Could I take you to dinner?" he blurted.

"Not tonight. Perhaps soon."

"Does that mean no?"

She shook her head deliberately.

"How did you know I was in Viet Nam?"

"I heard you talking to Tony and showing your tattoo. What does it say?"

He rolled up his sleeve. "You can't complain about that."

She sighed. "Good Conduct. I don't really understand it, but it doesn't seem so bad. Call me."

"Would you still be willing to have dinner with me if it'd said Death Before Dishonor?"

"No."

ON the way across town, the radio news told him Joost ter Braak, the Dutch opera impresario, had agreed at last to come to L.A. A garbage strike was starting in the morning. A chemical spill had forced the evacuation of most of El Monte. Two big-rigs had overturned in the East L.A. interchange, tying up four freeways. The usual slow motion urban apocalypse. There was nothing about Senora Beltran's body drifting down the L.A. River. Perhaps it hadn't inconvenienced enough people, he thought.

The temperature needle rode just below the H, not dangerous yet, something they couldn't get quite right about the thermostat that was still okay as long as he added fluid every other day. Chrysler dealers cringed when they saw the old AMC Concord coming, an orphan nobody wanted to fix.

Up ahead dark smoke plumed straight up a hundred feet and then sheared off inland, and helicopters circled and circled the pillar like fearful votives checking to see if the gods were accepting the offering. The street was blocked by a big ladder truck that was just setting up and he had to detour around the burning "Swap Meet," quotes included, that had once been a block of main street shops but had had the in-between walls knocked through. The windows had been painted over and the signs were for things he didn't recognize: *alfombras, mimados, tejados, maderaje.*

People massed on the side street where a large gorilla bobbed and bowed at the waist beside the door. As he watched, a tongue of flame blew out the glass door and licked into the gorilla's synthetic brown hair. He slowed to a crawl to watch the whole animal flame up like dry brush and within seconds the metal armature showed through, still bobbing away welcomingly. An air horn bleated once behind to chase him on so a pumper could get through.

He felt the childish excitement of fire—treading so near danger and extinction, or was it just the transformation of the ordinary into spectacle? No one gave enough credit to the simple fear of boredom as a motivator. He'd once tracked down a runaway girl to a party flat in the Valley where kids were shoving needles and carpet tacks and even roofing nails through their ears and navels and nipples. He knew a fair amount about disappointment, but he wondered how anyone ever got that bored.

It was late afternoon when he got off the freeway on

La Cienega. He passed an old apartment building that had caught his eye long ago. It had been abandoned, boarded up, then had had the boards ripped off and street kids had been living in it for months, covering it with graffiti. The most prominent sign, over the entrance, said *You're Fucked We're Your Future*.

Maybe so, he thought.

MARLENA'S UPS note was taped to his office door, but she had gone home so he went in and hunted in the debris for his phone. It wasn't that hard for a detective. He went to the wall outlet, picked up the cord and yanked on it until the phone emerged from the litter, trailing its handset.

"It's not really UPS. I just used their notepad, *querido*. A messenger brought a package."

"Will you come open up and get it for me?"

"I brought it home with me. You can get it when you come and have a drink."

"I see. You sure there's a package?"

"It's about the size of a stack of screenplays. I see a lot of them."

A chill went up his back.

"I want you to take the package out into the middle of your back yard and leave it there."

"What do you—?"

"Just do it for me, and then come back in the house, okay? I'll be there in ten minutes."

"Okay, Jack."

FIRST he lobbed an old brick onto it from about fifty feet away, and when nothing happened he looked it over more closely, without touching it. Marlena Cruz waited behind a flimsy garden shed that probably wouldn't have helped much, clutching a small hairless dog that was mewling away like a rodent. It was a brown manila package with his name on it and no return address, about eight inches thick. He got some rope and duct tape out of his car and taped the rope thoroughly to one end of the package. Then he taped the other end to a fence post and, beginning to feel foolish, he stood at the far end of the yard and yanked the package open. The brown paper tore noisily and a wad of papers spilled onto the lawn.

So much for sapper training.

"I'm glad it wasn't an admirer sending you a porcelain chotchke," she said.

"So am I," he said. "For sure."

He carried the papers indoors and set them on the rickety Danish modern coffee table, the only surface not already covered by her own chotchkes, porcelain dogs, wood and plaster dogs, aluminum dogs, large flocked floor-sitting dogs from Tijuana and small blown glass dogs from the county fair. The top quarter of the stack of documents was a single edge-bound booklet and the rest was loose papers.

"Aren't you going to look?"

"Not just now."

"I'll never figure you out," she sighed.

"Who brought the package?"

"A kid on a bike. Maybe twelve years old."

"Somebody from the neighborhood? Would you recognize him?"

"Probably. He had one of those funny bicycles kids have with the high handlebars, and he had a wicker basket on it. You don't see that so much."

"Keep your eye out for him."

She brought him a scotch with ice, stood behind him and began to massage his neck and shoulders. He had never told her he didn't drink; it involved too much explanation. He set the glass in front of himself and stared at the ice cubes bobbing to the surface.

"You look worn out tonight. Did you have a bad day?" She was much less ornery at home, or maybe it was being in heat.

It would have been great to drink it. "Not as bad as the Beltrans. They found her dead, drowned in the river."

"Ooh, I'm sorry. Did you see the boy?"

"He took it like a warrior, while anyone was watching. Then he cried. I wish city kids didn't have to grow up so fast. It's like a huge social experiment in forced breeding. All the middle tones will be gone in a generation. We won't even understand what a gentle smile is."

"Poor baby."

She ran her hands softly along his neck, dragging a nail, and his hair stood on end. He hadn't made up his mind how to get out of there before she got too far. His sense of the pattern in his life had been disrupted somehow, and he wasn't sure how to get it back. The dog was making rapid squeaking sounds and seemed to be trying to mount his shoe.

"Fidel, *stop* that."

She threw a small sofa pillow at the dog. The thing yelped and raced off into the house.

"Fidel?" he said.

"In Spanish it is common. It might not be referring to Castro."

"But it does?"

"Sure. I had Raul and Che, too, but Raul got distemper and Che ran in front of a Sparkletts truck and got run over."

"Your house is a holocaust for the Cuban Revolution."

She came around the sofa and curled up next to him.
"I like Cuba. Every Hispanic does a little, maybe se-
cretly, except the exiles. They thumbed their nose at Uncle Sam and they got free health care."

"The gays don't like it so much," he said.

"What do you care? This isn't for men, is it?" Her
hand rested on his penis, as it began to swell under his
trousers, then she kneaded him softly.

"You've never been quite so forward," he said.

"You keep slipping away. I want you, Jack. Please
don't make me ashamed." She bent forward and closed
her lips over the lump in his trousers, and he leaned
back, shocked not by her actions but her words. Had he
shamed her before, by diplomatically evading her bedroom?

It was strange how things happened. You drifted from
day to day, and months went by, years, then all of a
sudden, without you willing it, a change came up. He
knew he was going to go through with it now, but he
hadn't been thinking along this line at all. If he'd been
thinking this way, it was about a slim nervous ex-nun.

Unbuttoning the back of her dress, he found her
stockiness quite attractive. Then she was up against him
and they were exchanging very wet kisses.

"Slow, slow," he said. "We're not kids. We've got
all night."

"It's been too long," she said. The dog whined in
the doorway, and they went into the bedroom and shut
Fidel out.

There were ruffles on the bed and more decorative
dogs on various surfaces, a thousand tiny censorious
eyes on him. Her thick-strap brassiere released enormous
brown breasts that actually weighed heavy in his hands.

As they tumbled into the four-poster, his mind raced
against his will, spinning off into some strange realm.

He imagined the two of them moving out of the city to start a dog-breeding ranch somewhere up in Canyon Country. Not the little yippy dogs, but shepherds and danes and collies. They could sell the dogs to people who turned off Highway 14 in their station wagons on the way to the Antelope Valley, and Maeve would come out alternate weekends to help train the smarter shepherds as seeing-eye dogs.

She got both hands on his penis, rubbing it against herself as she knelt over him, and he imagined the lazy moon-lit nights when they had finally grown used to the incessant howling and baying. At the end of the year, they would sit rocking on the long porch and he would say, *The dogs have been good to us.* She said something and he felt her fingernails scrabbling at his back. Only toward the end when they were both finally quieting down did he notice the persistent scratching at the door. She was very brown everywhere and smelled strong and wonderful and tasted salty.

"It doesn't mean you have to marry me," she said, pounding the pillow under her head. "It's just good."

"You'd better tell that to Fidel. He's going crazy with jealousy."

The volume came up when he opened the door, the dog yipping away at him as he walked past to the coffee table in her bathrobe. He lifted the bound volume. "To Mr. L" was written on a note taped to the cover in fat magic marker letters.

It was a report labeled "Babylonian Opera House and Performance Center." He recognized the artist's sketch on the cover, the 1000-yard-long facade of the Samson Rubber Company, a faux Babylonian temple along the L.A. River, just another of L.A.'s vernacular buildings like the Brown Derby and the giant donut. Latterly it had been Uniroyal and then it had sat derelict and decaying in the far corner of Cahuenga for twenty years, bas reliefs of striding middle eastern kings spalling away under the graffiti.

Joost ter Braak, he thought, have they told you about this? He read the *Times* regularly, and this plan to re-develop the rubber temple was a famous civic secret, known to everyone, never whispered in public. The rest of the stack included financing plans worked out by the Basin Redevelopment Agency, memos from city officials, business plans and county department documents that would take him a lifetime to digest.

Who, he thought, wanted an opera house badly, and who didn't? And who on earth would kill for it?

6

TO MAKE YOU LOOK THE WRONG WAY

DRIVING DOWN TOWARD PLAYA VISTA INTO THE MORNING overcast, he passed a tall man strolling along Jefferson in white bucks, carrying a banjo, and he wondered if the man had fallen asleep in a time vault for thirty or forty years. L.A. was like that. On his left bulldozers were reshaping the last open wetlands for a big new plantation of condos.

Overlooking the site was the long cliff of Westchester, the south bank of the historic floodplain of the L.A. River until a big storm in the middle of the 19th century had diverted the main flow south toward Long Beach to leave only Ballona Creek flowing west. Few people in L.A. noticed the natural features that were still there beneath the grid of streets—like the slope a mile north at Rose that had been the north bank of the floodplain. He had once enjoyed knowing things like that, the broken geography under the asphalt and the lost flora and fauna, it was like getting a leg up on the massive denial that the city feasted on, but he was becoming tired of knowing too many things that did him no good.

The art school where Lewis taught one day a week was a post-modern assemblage of tinkertoys and kitsch,

like the leftovers from several real buildings, and he
parked right in front and tried not to look at all the in-
your-face ugliness. Too many opinions, he thought. You
didn't need to carry them around with you. You could
probably make up as much as you needed as you went
along.

"Lousy overcast," he said to the blonde secretary.
She eyed him suspiciously.

"I'd like to leave some stuff for Mike Lewis."

"He shares a box with the grad R.A.s." She nodded
to a rabbit-warren of boxes against the wall. The big one
marked *RA's*—somebody was taking no chances with
the apostrophe—was stuffed.

"It appears to be full."

She took a long time seconding his opinion. "You
can't leave it on the counter. It's against policy to leave
mail on the counter." She broke off, as if that settled it.

"Perhaps if we put our heads together," he said
slowly, "we can come up with a solution to this problem."

"He's not in today." She had rheumy eyes and he
wondered if she was on some kind of slow-down drug.
"He's in his office tomorrow at one."

Mommas always told you that you got farther with
politeness. "Is there some way I could leave a package
this size for him? Just *theoretically* speaking."

"I can't take the responsibility for accepting something."

"What if you unlock his office door and leave it on
his desk?"

"I'm not authorized to do that."

"Is there someone who can?"

"Not now."

He had a vision of this going on forever, an endless
series of cavils and quoted regulations, their hair grow-

ing out and out over the years like Einstein's until it
filled every crevice of the office.

"What if I sat down here, poured gasoline over myself and lit it?"

She glared.

He left the office and circled the building. In the back
corner of the small campus he found a doublewide house
trailer with *Custodial* over the open door. Inside, a squat
Latino was loading bottles and cans onto a rolling cart.

"*Compañero*, I'm trying to leave some papers for
Mike Lewis who teaches here. I'm having a little trouble
with the Dragon Lady."

There was a hint of a smile hovering at the corner of
the man's lip. Jack Liffey tucked a ten-dollar bill into
the packet of papers.

"Do you think you could put it in his room for me?"

The janitor looked around quickly and then tucked
the packet under some rags on the bottom of the cart.

"Is this a good place to work?" Liffey asked.

The janitor shrugged. "I had my own land in El Sal-
vador. I didn't hold my hat in my hand."

"I hope you get your land back, senor. *Gracias.*"

"*De nada.*"

Driving away, he saw a hillock of black trash bags
piled in the corner of a mini-mall and he remembered
the garbage strike. Flies were already dancing in cele-
bration. It would only get worse.

He wondered if you could equate having your own
land to having a secure job with a window office and a
good salary, working alongside a few people you respected, doing something you were good at and recognized for being good at. Neither one had turned out to
have much of a future.

On the other side of Jefferson three cop cars were
askew and two old Mustangs were stopped with their

doors open, a half dozen young black men sitting hand-cuffed on the curb. The cop cars were LAPD and a helicopter was circling, too, in case the suspects tried to levitate. Then he noticed one man being stripped by two of the cops, a pistol to his head. He had a vision of gang rape by the police, with the rest of the city commuting past to work, pretending not to see.

The arrest scene didn't matter, not really. The black trash bags didn't matter either. The Dragon Lady in the office. The foam cups fouling the concrete river. Gorillas on fire. That was the problem, letting your attention be diverted by what didn't matter, getting scared by it, fouling up your consciousness with it. The world was getting fuller and fuller of stuff that didn't matter. Maybe he could help the kid, Tony. That might be something that mattered.

He dreaded seeing the mess in his office again but he had to dig out Chris Johnson's phone number. He was a former computer hacker and phone phreak who'd turned to designing video games a half jump ahead of the techno-cops from AT&T who'd taken a dim view of his work. Two years earlier a radio station had offered an old Porsche 501 to the 97th caller and Chris had blown away their tie line and placed every call from 50 through 97, just for good measure.

The air over the city smelled sweet for some reason, like animal fodder, as he got back to his own mini-mall. Perhaps it was a leftover of the rain. He smiled at Marlena sweeping her walk as he drove past to park in back and she blew him a kiss.

His office door was standing open again and he sighed. Maybe the burglars had come back and tidied it for him. His sarcasm abandoned him abruptly when he entered and saw the man standing in the shadows in the room.

"Worst mess I ever saw sans the aid of hooch," the man drawled. "Looks like you turpentined a couple cats in here, Jack."

He wore a big white cowboy hat and tooled boots, but he was small and weaselly and didn't seem to belong in them. His body shifted rhythmically, like a mongoose in front of a cobra. Jack Liffey tried to remember exactly where his guns were. The Dreyse was in the car and the Ballester Molina he'd taken home. He wondered if he should bolt.

"You mind telling me why you're in my office?"

"I want you to think on the last couple days, pardner." He sat down in the swivel chair and a gray light caught his face. Something was wrong with his eyes. "Somebody brought you something, I think."

"A black figurine," Jack Liffey said. "A bird of some sort."

He calculated he could be out of the room in half a second, and then he felt something hard in his back, the size of a gun and with what felt like a lot of mass. A *big* gun.

"We know you're smart as a cuttin' horse. Just keep still." A hand felt expertly down his legs, up hard enough in his crotch to cause a twinge, across the small of his back and under his arms. "I know you, you done some ridin' and ropin' in the big Nam, think you can't be scared no more, but don't you believe it."

The Cowboy swiveled back and forth in a restless way. Liffey wondered if the one behind him was the dangerous one. He was shoved all of a sudden from the side and he stumbled into a corner of the office away from the door. The other man filled the doorway backlit so all you could see was that he was big, a feature player, but without the gaudy clothing of the other man. He carried a little Mac-11 spray gun with the 32-shot magazine. There were sure a lot of guns about.

"You've got me confused with somebody else. I scare easy."

The Cowboy took a hand-rolled out of his shirt pocket and lit it with a wooden match. The smell was unmistakably dope. He sucked deep and held it a long time, smiling. He didn't seem very interested in talking to Jack Liffey.

The big man stooped and picked up a little battery radio and tested it. A jazz station came on and he held it away from his ear as if it had stung him.

"It's your dime," Liffey said.

"Well, you're just right upholstered with impatience, ain't you?"

The big man found an oldies station and seemed to relax as some Stones came on, "Wild Horses." Couldn't drag him away.

"I got stuff to do today," Jack Liffey said. "So why don't you guys come back some other time and we'll talk about whatever you've got on your mind." If they were going to shoot him they'd have done it.

"You shore don't use all your kindlin' gettin' your fire started up. I want you to know we ain't kiddin' around here. The men we work for pay more in sales tax on a bad day than you got in the world, and you don't even cut their shadow. Fact you'd have to stand in the same place twice just to cast a shadow they could see."

The gaudy patter annoyed him, but it didn't seem like a good time to complain about it.

"We don't care what you do with the stuff you got, we just don't care, because you don't amount to grease on a flapjack. But don't make us care." The Cowboy took out his own pistol now, a little .32 that belonged in a purse.

The big man was behind him again and suddenly Jack Liffey's hand was wrenched behind him and then he heard the screech of cloth tearing and his wrists were being tied together with what felt like duct tape as the Stones sang on.

"We're not in this fuckin' business to have to give the same message twice, you understand? That Spic cunt fell in the river. That's the end of it. You understand that?"

"Sure, uh-huh. I'm on top of it."

The big man thrust his knees suddenly into the backs of Jack Liffey's knees. It was an old playground trick, but if you weren't ready for it, there was nothing you could do but go down hard. He managed to break his fall a bit by angling his weight so his hip and shoulder hit at the same time. The big man taped his ankles, then flipped him over onto his back so he lay uncomfortably on the lump of his tied hands and taped his mouth.

The Cowboy stooped and dragged the little purse automatic across Liffey's cheek like a straight razor. "You best save your breath now for breathin'. Our friend here's meaner 'n a sheared sheep."

He tore open Jack Liffey's shirt, little pearl buttons spinning away on the linoleum as the cool air hit his belly. He could see the big man's shoes, Redwing engineer boots that badly needed oil on the scuffs. The music came up loud on the radio, Jim Morrison croon-talking his way through "The End."

Can you picture what will be, so limitless and free?

From somewhere the big man produced a writhing snake, a big diamondback rattlesnake. He held it hard behind the head so the open jaws couldn't get at his fat fingers, and he let the tail dangle over Jack Liffey's bare stomach, the rattle just grazing gooseflesh. It rattled once vigorously and then just shivered, a light grating sound like sheets of paper rubbing over one another. He could only hear it in lulls in the music.

All the children are insane, waiting for the summer rain.

''The spic cunt, she had an accident. She had cooties. Believe it.''

His body went tense and his chest arched up. The big man lowered the snake so the body wound back and forth across Jack Liffey's bare chest. His neck ached with the effort of holding his head up to see. The snake was heavy and cool, as if dead, but of course it was cold blooded.

The killer awoke before dawn. He put his boots on.

If he got any more tense he would explode. The big man lowered the snake's head and it went out of sight behind a coil. He could see up close that the diamond markings were made up of the whitened tips of diagonal rows of scales. The big man withdrew his hand gingerly and the snake writhed slightly. It seemed to be resting before making up its mind what to do, the rattle quivering.

The long throbbing bell-like organ solo started up.

''Bye now.''

He saw their feet withdraw as one of the coils of the snake flexed lightly and resettled across his belly. He wondered if its strike was always fatal or if it would just make him very sick. He remembered being told to cut crosshatches with a razor and suck out the poison, and then he remembered being told that that was no longer the conventional wisdom, that cutting crosshatches would only spread the venom more rapidly. He thought they made snakebite kits with little rubber suction cups, but it was academic because he didn't have a snakebite kit. He was sweating with the strain.

The snake rose and fell with his breathing but all its

other motions seemed to damp down. Most of its weight hung to the right side of his chest and he contemplated rolling slowly in that direction to encourage a departure, but wondered if disturbing the perch would touch off a strike. The strain got to him and he let his neck fall back, but he couldn't stand not seeing for long.

Jack Liffey began to rotate his trunk to the right by infinitesimal stages. The reptile's scales did not seem to have much bite on his flesh, and when he got to 45 degrees he could sense the snake beginning to move.

The West is the best. The West is the best.

The snake slid to the floor in a rush and Jack Liffey spun and rolled away in the opposite direction, picturing the rattler coming alert the moment it touched down and coming after him. He bucked and writhed, hit his head hard on the corner of his desk and finally wrenched his bound hands over his buttocks and brought them in front of himself for defense.

The snake hadn't moved an inch. It lay in some sort of defensive posture with its head aimed square at where Jack Liffey waited.

He ripped the tape off his mouth, then tore at the duct tape with his teeth and finally twisted his hands free, scrabbling for a weapon. A baseball bat would be perfect, but he didn't have a baseball bat. He settled for a heavy gray homemade vase one of his low-paying customers had given him in gratitude.

The snake seemed to be mesmerized, and all at once Jack Liffey got mad and threw down the vase. He got to his feet, still bound at the ankles, and hopped forward until he came down hard on the snake's head several times. It made no effort to avoid him, and there was a solid gummy resistance under his shoes like stepping on a hose.

It was some kind of rubber snake and they'd made

him look like an idiot. Which was the point. His vision
went red. To make you look the wrong way, to make
you afraid of the thing that was irrelevant, the thing that
was coming from the wrong place.

He tore the tape off his ankles and waited for his heart
to slow down.

The end of nights we tried to die. This is the end.

He knew he was way over his head now, up against
some really dangerous people, but none of that mattered.
They had fucked with his self-esteem.

7

THE DEFORMATION OF SURFACES

A SMOLDER OF ANGER RODE WITH HIM AND IT FLARED irrationally when a policeman made a brusque two-hand pushing gesture to get his car to pull wider. For a millisecond he pictured driving the cop down, sending him topsy-turvy. But the reason for the detour was clear enough—a poultry truck had overturned and was burning across most of the road.

He'd spent the night nursing images of the Cowboy and the snake and trying to think himself into an alternate universe where he had behaved bravely and well. It was no use.

Chickens scurried past, a few actually on fire. Pedestrians chased them down, some laughing like children and others in an earnest of charity. He cranked the window down and could hear the cacophony of the chickens still in the truck, driven to an awareness of their danger. The driver tugged heroically on battery cage doors, freeing as many birds as he could, grabbing and flinging them away from him. A dusting of feathers hung in the air and one of the burning chickens fluttered up onto the Concord's hood with a tremendous will of wingbeats. The bird hit the glass and implored his comfort with hard yellow eyes for just an instant, and then it was gone, leaving a sad aftertaste of cruelty in the air. His psyche had no room to sympathize with chickens.

From a poultry point of view, he thought, the holocaust would be remembered for generations, retold and embellished until at last it became only a dim folk tale in the chicken memory. The day the iron beast caught fire and devoured our grandmothers. The cop pointed straight at him like death in a Swedish movie and waved him on.

And at his very worst the night before, Kathy had called. His child support was late.

I loved you so damn much once, Jack, I loved you to drive me to distraction. I can't believe it. I used to say it all the time. Imagine that. We were so close there for so long, I just can't believe it any more. I won't let myself get that close to anyone any more, I won't. I haven't. Remember that time I hit you with the ladle? Remember? I broke your collarbone.

Sure, he remembered.

What was I mad about, I can't remember?

He didn't know either but he must have deserved it.

She wouldn't let him talk to Maeve.

No money, no rights, Jack. That's the bottom line in this household. No money, no rights.

It was the American credo, for sure.

Tony was working out with his homemade weights when Jack Liffey drove up. He was doing curls in a frenzy, pumping away like a machine gone amok. Either it was a kind of aerobic training or the boy was working out his emotions. Across the street a handful of older boys with bandannas on their foreheads poked under the hood of a '62 Chevy low-rider. A woman was watering something in the tiny grotto. He wondered if they made

Chia-pet Marys, and then decided it was a pretty mean thought.

Jack Liffey went around to the back where Tony was huffing and puffing.

"*Hola*, T-Bell," he said.

The boy noticed him but didn't break his pace. He'd be a real hard one some day if nothing intervened. At the end of the set, he slammed down the pipe with its concrete cans.

"Grandma wants to see you."

"In a minute. I came to see you."

The boy picked up a towel, wiped his forehead off and tossed it back in the corner like a tennis player between sets.

Two dogs came along the weeds gnarring at one another, the bigger one backing up in apprehension. The bigger was a mongrel but it had the fat strong mouth of a rottweiler. The smaller looked like a white coyote and had a coyote way of trying to get sideways.

"Jaime! *Ven!*"

The boy bolted and got between the dogs, kicking out at the bigger one.

"*Ve! Ve!* Fuck off!"

He grabbed the collar of the frenzied white dog with both hands and held it back. Jack Liffey walked straight at the rottweiler. "Get lost!"

By some miracle the rottweiler barked once and then fled. Liffey knelt beside the white dog. The eyes were wild. The dog was really wired and couldn't get itself down.

"He's part coyote, isn't he?"

"I think so. My dad brought him from Arizona."

"When was that?" Liffey ran his hand down the dog's chest from the neck down between the forelegs, over and over, soothing the animal. The breeder's trick worked like a charm, and the dog stiffened up to stillness and then gradually relaxed.

"I don't know."

"Is he in Arizona now? Your dad."

The boy didn't answer. It was a touchy subject.

"Try this if he gets wild. No dog can resist it."

"We have to put him on a chain at night or he goes hunting for cats."

They both fell silent for a moment.

"Do you know what a BMW M3 is?" Jack Liffey asked.

The boy nodded, but just to make sure he added, "With all the skirts and spoilers and the lumpy fenders sticking out."

"Sure, I know."

As far as Liffey knew, nobody imported them back then, the bored-out engines couldn't make the smog regulations. They were brought in special order and modified at great expense.

"It's all black, black chrome, and blacked-out glass. Do you ever see anything like that around town here?"

The boy shook his head. "You kidding? Only nigger dope dealers drive that thing."

"Say black men. For me. Some yuppies have them, too, and others." It had been in the lot outside his office before he ran into the Cowboy and it had been gone when he came down. And he remembered seeing it the morning of the break-in. "Keep your eye out and see if you can find out who has one."

"Is this about my mom?"

"It might be."

"I get the C-60 Locos to find it, man. We blow him away."

"I said 'might.' Don't spook him. Just find out who it is. Let's talk to your grandma."

Senora Schuler was in the kitchen, spreading masa with her hands on a large sheet of plywood. Her eyes were red-rimmed and she greeted him with great dignity. Immediately she washed her hands and offered him coffee. He could see it was not in her nature to chat with him in the kitchen, as a Midwest farm wife might have. She would have felt it rude, so he waited with the boy on the worn brocade sofa. The room had been tidied since the relatives and police had gone, but it looked even more cluttered, with every space taken up by something, photos, china, a crucifix, a book. It gave him an odd feeling of rigidity, like a world that would never have room for something new.

She brought a brass tray with coffee and sugar-cookies.

"She wants to thank you for coming back," the boy translated "And she wants to hire you to find who killed mama. She doesn't think the police will try very hard."

"Does she have some reason for thinking that?"

"Does she need to?"

That was the boy's reply, a twelve-year-old's world-size cynicism, and it might have masked an infinity of real issues.

"Ask her, please."

The woman flicked her eyebrows once and poured out the coffee. She spoke for a while. "She has a feeling, she says. Ahm ... the cop who is half Mexican isn't very honest. And the other doesn't count."

"Is she just judging on her experience of the Hermosillo police? Or does she have a reason for disliking Lieutenant Zuniga?"

She stared at the carpet for a long time.

"She says he took things without asking. Something from under the bed and some papers from mama's drawer." The boy indicated the chest built into the wall with a mirror over it, a kind of sideboard. "It was her desk."

The coffee was strong and good. He would have to spend some time going through what was left in the drawer, but presumably if there was something interesting, it was in a manila folder on Zuniga's desk. What did people keep under the bed?

"Grandma owns land in a village outside Hermosillo. If a lot of money is necessary to pay you, she can sell the land and get it."

"I've already hired myself." He smiled. "Remember, I'm *simpatico*. How big was the thing that was under the bed?"

The old woman shrugged. She made hand gestures that indicated it could have been anything from a missing earring to a smallish book. He made a mental note to look under all the beds and under the stuffed furniture.

He drank up and asked permission to look over the house himself and use the phone.

A dial phone was in a built-in plastered alcove in the hall. He hadn't seen a dial in years. "Art Castro, please."

Castro was a real detective, in a big agency with a secretary and a lot of electronic toys. Rosewood Agency, home office Cincinnati, where they once supplied strikebreakers to all the bigger robber barons. They even had a big eye painted on the door.

"May I tell him who's calling?"

"No."

He had no secrets, he just hated the formula, and she probably made him listen to the elevator music longer than normal on account of it.

"Hello, who is this?"

"This is Jack Liffey, Art."

"Next time why don't you give your name. You got Ellen really steamed."

"It's good for her. Besides, I don't want you being out to old friends."

There was an electronic squawk. "This is Art Castro's voice mail. Please leave a message."

"I swear to god, Art, if you've actually punched me over to voice mail, I'll come down there and make you eat the telephone."

"Just a joke, Jack. Lighten up." Over the phone, there was a sudden rattle of tinny machine gun fire, then an ambulance siren, finally a fart. "Somebody gave me this battery thing from a funny store."

Liffey described the Cowboy and his pal in detail, and the car. "You know anybody like that on the east side?"

"Jeez, the east side of what? What's in it for me?"

"Maybe I can get you a sublease on the case. There seems to be some money here. You don't have to catch these guys, just identify them."

"Man, I can tell there's something there to be afraid of and you don't care if I'm afraid or not."

"Hell, Art, you got all the troops. When the going gets tough, the tough get toys."

"East side, huh? The *gabacho* cowboy sounds more like Canyon Country. But, okay, I'll ask a couple gentlemen I know. Know anything about the license plate?"

"I don't even know if it had one. I don't think there was one in front, where I saw, but I wasn't paying attention."

"That's how you get hurt, my friend."

"You get hurt being a wiseass. I'll be in touch."

Of course he should have noticed the license plate. And the guy should have been looking up when the meteor came in low, too. You couldn't watch everything.

It was only in the movies that the detective noticed the patch of red dust on the lounger's boots. The rest of the guys were busy watching women with big breasts or somebody in a flashy shirt or a beautiful blue sky. Maybe he'd always be an out-of-work technical writer.

The drawer, actually two drawers, didn't help much. One was all bills and receipts, as if she had been saving up to file a Schedule C. Electricity, cable TV, gas, lots of grocery bills, phone. He set the phone bills aside, made sure all the recent ones were there, in case he wanted to look over the long distance numbers later. The other drawer was a tidy school desk, with class notes in spiral books and some loose papers in a Pee-Chee. They still made Pee-Chees, he thought with wonder, with the same sprinter heading for the tape. And still a white guy, the sprinter, as if the artist had never seen a real track meet.

History of Religion. Historiography. Twentieth Century American. Russian. Europe after 1400. Labor History. Pre-Columbian Americas. And some other subjects, English Literature and Drama. Sociology. Anthropology. What *was* the difference between sociology and anthropology? The lives of white people, the lives of dark people? Her notes were all in a tidy hand and all in complete sentences.

Under Tony's bed there was a dog-toy, a knot of leather like a bone, nothing under the other one. There were only the two bedrooms.

When he was done, Tony was gone. Senora Schuler had retreated to the kitchen where she was wrapping masa in corn husks and he said goodbye. She held up one hand, as if she wanted to say something. They were both frustrated by the languages. Why had he always put off learning Spanish? Why had he taken Latin in high school? *Latin!* So now he could talk to old priests and read prescriptions.

"Take very careful," she said.

"*Si, cuidado. Gracias,*" he said. He hadn't told her about the snake.

FIFTEEN minutes later he was peering in the glass door at the Catholic Liberation House, at all the empty desks in the storefront. The only person there was the earnest kid in the Pendleton, typing with two fingers like a cop. Most of the dismembered car in the street had been hauled away, though the seats and part of the dash had been left attached to the chassis for some reason, like the setup for a cheap play.

"Eleanor Ong here?" The last name, as if there were a lot of other Eleanors he might be asking about. Jack Liffey noticed that the cops had been. All the drawers of Consuela Beltran's desk had been sealed up with yellow tape.

"She's in the kitchen." The boy nodded to the inner door and Liffey thought he sensed the boy's irritation. He went in to find an untidy hallway, bikes, coats on pegs, an aluminum walker. He guessed left and found an equally untidy kitchen.

"You shouldn't see this," she said. *This* was the fact she was frying slices of Oscar Mayer baloney.

He was surprised, by the baloney and the getup. Since she'd worn a gypsy dress the first time, he expected her to be in something like that always, but she wore a tight green leotard and black jeans. She was thinner than he remembered, but that might have been the contrast to Marlena. It wasn't a value judgment, even deep in his head. Marlena's body had been a lot of fun. His heart was light. How was it that being attracted to one woman could make you attracted to another one at almost the same time? The way Eleanor Ong's body moved under the leotard was fabulous.

"Sometimes I slice a crumb doughnut," he said, "and make a swiss cheese crumb doughnut sandwich."

She laughed. "In the convent, we'd pool our mad money once in a while and buy a packet of baloney and do this. One of the sisters grew up in working class Philadelphia and apparently this is popular there. I got a real taste for it. Did you really make cheese and doughnut sandwiches?"

"No, but I thought it would make you feel better."

She laughed again. "I love the way they curl up and you sort of push them back down until you sear a ring and then flip them over and they invert themselves like some kind of sea anemone. There must be some branch of physics that explains it."

"Topology," he said.

She glanced up. "Seriously?"

"It's the study of the deformation of surfaces."

"I never know when you're serious."

"I'm serious enough about taking you to dinner."

"Not tonight, but maybe soon."

Her voice had dropped a tone. She piled the baloney onto a slice of wheat bread, slapped another slice of bread on top and had a little fun with the way it resisted and tried to rise up.

"Shouldn't play with your food," he said.

"Would you like some?"

"I'll wait for the pickle ice cream. Did Senora Beltran ever talk about the big Samson Rubber building?"

"Not that I remember."

"Did it come up in the city council campaign?"

"Not really, but it was the ghost at the feast that you don't talk about. There's been hints about rebuilding it as an opera house for years. The Slow Growth people were probably in favor because it was a prestige project and developing it would supplant a lot of crowded Latino homes and would soak up a lot of redevelopment money that ought to go to low-cost housing. The community people were probably against it for about the same reasons. Prestige only meant prestige for the Anglo establishment in downtown L.A. Not many people here hum Figaro. Are you sure you wouldn't like something?''

''No thanks.''

She sat down at the scarred kitchen table with a glass of milk and began to eat.

''How does it stand about the opera house?'' he asked.

''I don't know. There's nothing public, just the rumors.''

''You know,'' he said, ''the papers say some muckymuck opera impresario has decided to come to L.A. Maybe he knows something we don't. How strong would the opposition to the opera house be?''

''It doesn't seem to me that big an issue. Maybe it would heat up if it meant diverting a serious amount of redevelopment money. You should talk to Xavier Gallegos. He's the savviest guy in the neighborhood organization.''

''If you'll get me his number.'' Cars meant nothing to her, but he described the Cowboy and what he could of the Cowboy's buddy. ''Has anyone like that been around here?''

She shook her head. ''Did you ask Jonathan?''

''Is that the kid out front?''

''The kid is almost twenty.''

''I sense he doesn't really want to talk to me, not since I got chummy with you, anyway.''

She took some time chewing, as if thinking about the food.

"It isn't surprising he'd be smitten," Jack Liffey said.

"Let it go right now, Jack."

"You did tell me you weren't still a virgin."

"Isn't that sort of an impertinent thing to say?"

"You take pains to be an impertinent sort of woman."

"Perhaps we'll talk about it again when you know me better."

"I look forward to it. In the meantime, if those guys show up, please don't antagonize them. They've got a real mean streak."

8

WINNING MAKES YOU STUPID

FOR A MINUTE THERE, HE'D FELT AN UNREASONING HAPPI-
ness as he drove out Atlantic and crossed the straight
scar of the L.A. River, heading toward Samson Rubber.
He felt as if he'd fallen out of time and space. Something
that he didn't want to look at too closely was cheering
him up. Not looking was probably the key.

The mood frayed as he glanced off the bridge just
across the river. In a waste of industrial land, a few
homeless had set up an encampment of old sofas and
refrigerator boxes, and in the sea of mud two enraged
old men were dueling with prosthetic arms. The fluorescent pink arms with shiny pincer-hooks slammed into
one another like sabers. When he stopped the car, he
could hear the clack of plastic on plastic. The hairy filthy
men circled one another, shouting and feinting, and he
heard another blow and a bellow of pain. No one was
too far gone to partake of the human condition.

He parked opposite the rubber factory, so big and tall
that it was really a walled city. There were watch towers
in the corners and every fifty yards, with toothy battlements all along. The walls had Babylonian warriors in
relief, striding kilted into battle, or riding war chariots.

It was far too big to be just an opera house. Perhaps it was meant to contain a number of theaters, maybe even enclosed parking and shops. Opera City, Opera Mall, with guards along the battlements to fire on the massed poor and other non-consumers.

Who would kill to transform the ruin? Or prevent it? It seemed ridiculous.

Most of the graffiti had been painted out, but time had not been kind to the plaster walls that had been grooved to imitate sandstone blocks. Sections had fallen away raggedly, like flayed skin. He saw one hole up high that went on through, past roof trusses to the blue sky beyond.

Jack Liffey went very still and broke into a cold sweat. Waylaid by the sight. He hadn't even thought about it for years. He'd been playing by himself in the hills above his home, trekking across the garbanzo bean fields to the open chaparral on the higher slopes. Without warning the earth had vanished to leave him falling through space, scraping one shoulder against something rough. Fortunately and unfortunately he had landed in water. Rainwater or crop water had collected in the abandoned glory hole to break his fall. But it was too deep for him to touch bottom and when he came up flailing there was nothing to grab onto. Far above him in the blackness there was a small oblong of blue sky.

Liffey squeezed his eyes shut. The blue had been too vivid, infinitely far. He had tried to scream back then but hadn't been able to. All he could do was tread water and try to force himself calm. He was a powerful swimmer. Eventually he found a toehold that held some of his weight and he dug away a shelf just above water level to grab on. He could rest for a few minutes, holding fiercely, and then tread water again. It was police dogs that found him nine hours later, after dark, just as he was about to lose it.

Jack Liffey pried his hands off the wheel and looked away. He counted backwards from fifty. They said you had to get right back on the horse, and he had. But he still hated swimming more than anything.

YOU know I signed a consent order.''

Chris Johnson lived in a little square stucco house that was out of place in the West Hollywood neighborhood of craftsman and Spanish bungalows. The original had probably burned down and this had been inserted like a later false tooth in a denture.

''This isn't much of a hack,'' Liffey said.

He was tall and handsome and so blond you could almost see through him. Johnson was an anarchist, a cyberpunk techno-hippie who just happened to look exactly like a Hitler youth, and he had a black girlfriend with dreadlocks who called herself Dot Matrix.

He was in sweats, striding and pumping at some kind of ski training machine, like the happy warrior in some cable infomercial. The machine made a herky-jerky grating sound. Amazingly, Johnson had once been drafted by the Forty-Niners as a wide receiver but he had walked out of training camp to get back to his keyboard and his hacking. He'd finally been caught and given eighteen months, suspended, for the ultimate transgression of charging his phone bill to the Republican National Committee. Suspended, as long as he stayed away from computers and never took the case off a telephone.

''You know, it's just an opera society. There's very little effort expended trying to steal so-and-so's score for Verdi.''

The court hadn't really been persuasive. The living room was filled with contraband apparatus, phone monitoring boxes, patch boxes, trunk line test sets, and a panel with looping oscilloscopes that Johnson called his time machine. There was the usual computer stuff, and several portable tool boxes labeled Black Bag 1, 2 and 3. Jack Liffey didn't even want to know what was in the bags. He picked up a gold Cross pen that was engraved *With the personal good wishes of Richard M. Nixon*, and he didn't want to know about that either.

"There shouldn't be much security."

Chris Johnson slowed his long-legged cross-country pace and then stopped. "They may not have anything on line." He gnashed his teeth theatrically. "Sorry, I'm in a bad mood today because Dot had her little brother in and he's a mouthy little shit."

Liffey smiled. "Bet he used some slang you'd never heard before."

"How'd you know? He called me a grebe-popper or something that sounded like that."

"Not being state-of-the-art is the only thing that gets your goat. I'd like to know if there's anything going on with plans for a new opera house."

"You're there, dude."

Still sweating, Johnson sat at an ordinary-looking computer console and launched an elaborate start-up. He was over thirty, but seeing him always reminded Jack Liffey of something in his own childhood, a feeling of inexhaustible possibilities, a promise that you were going to get to play outside after dusk. It was a feeling he'd once liked a lot, but lost somewhere. He let his eye drift along the books in Johnson's bookcase, almost all of which were tactical military histories. More of the man's sheer perversity. He picked up *Hell in a Very Small Place*.

"Why do you read this shit?"

"War is the purest form of football. The tactics are

right out there, and you've got a much better chance to cheat, and there's no disputing where the ball came down.''

"You were born in the wrong era.''

"Christ, I don't want to *fight* a war. People *shoot* at you. I just want to read about them. Look at General Giap. He learned from watching kittens. Retreat when the enemy is vigilant, attack when the enemy is looking the other way. What did you learn from your war? You don't talk about it much.''

"I learned to carry a clipboard so it always looks like you've got something to do.''

"That's not war. That's bureaucracy.''

"If you absolutely have to fight, stand near the guys who know what they're doing.''

"Better. Let me tell you what I've learned.''

He'd known this was coming.

Chris Johnson rocked in his swivel-chair and folded his hands in his lap happily. "Toward the end of the first world war, the German Army withdrew for a time from active combat. They pulled groups of NCOs from the front and retrained them in new tactics. They re-equiped their units with submachine guns and a whole new approach to the war. After all the years of trench war, the general staff had reinvented the attack in depth.''

He smiled in self-satisfaction, as if he had done the inventing himself.

"It was cavalry tactics on a grand scale. No more broad frontal assaults. They would mass at a single point and try to break through and then sweep on in to continue the attack from the flanks and rear of the enemy. It would demoralize and rout. It did, in fact. The Germans almost took Paris in 1918. It was only the arrival

of millions of fresh doughboys from America that lost
them the war.

''They'd invented the blitzkrieg, you see, but since
they lost the war, they were the only ones who noticed.
The French, who won, built the Maginot Line. Twenty
years later the German panzer divisions made the French
look stupid.''

He stopped and began to hammer at his keyboard.
''You know what that teaches me?''

Liffey decided to bite. ''What did that teach you?''

''Always talk to the losers. Winning makes you stupid and losing makes you smart.''

''No wonder you talk to me.''

He chuckled. ''Brecht said it, too: 'First the pain.
Then the idea.' Sit still and amuse yourself for a few
minutes. I'll jack into the net.''

He fiddled with his time machine and then keyed a
lot of numbers into the terminal, waiting while phones
dialed other phones. He got up to patch a few cables
behind the apparatus and went to another terminal. Once
in a while high spirits made him do a little dance between stations.

Jack Liffey took another book down at random, a
history of British commandos fighting with the partisans
in Yugoslavia during World War II. There were photos
of very thin men in khaki, arm-in-arm in piney mountains. Back then things seemed to matter. Nobody he'd
known in Viet Nam had cared a damn about the war.
There was a photo of Tito, smiling in the doorway of a
tent, and he thought of all the world leaders a half century back—Churchill and Roosevelt and Stalin and
DeGaulle and Mao. Nobody had any stature any more.
What had gone wrong?

He thumbed to a photo of Yugoslav guerrillas who
were leading away a squad of Germans with their hands

laced behind their heads. There would never be any more wars like that. They would be impersonal and technological, with men dancing at consoles just like Johnson, men at two or three removes from things tangible. Wars of *information* and *leverage*.

A printer started up across the room.

"No go," Johnson said. "They have no on-line databases. That's still the perfect form of data security against me, you know. But I can get you a couple of things. One of their PCs has a fax card and I managed to *persuade* the hard disk to cough up the last few weeks of faxes. I won't get them until down time tonight. Coming out now from Ma Bell is the last few months of their long distance calls."

"Is that it?"

He got a sly look all at once. "It's never it. I always hold a bit back. That's my edge."

Jack Liffey waited, but nothing else was forthcoming.

"Which general did you learn that from?"

"Napoleon. But then he's also the one who said espionage was useless." He grinned. "When you're winning, you don't need it and when you're losing you can't use it."

HE'D got off at the wrong ramp, City Terrace instead of Eastern, and now he was dead stuck in one of those mystery jams. Nothing had moved for ten minutes and people were getting out of their cars.

"What is it?"

"Dunno."

He got out, too, and drifted up the center of the street along with the other desultory urban pioneers. A few stood on their hoods, shielding their eyes like Remington bronzes. He saw a bit of smoke around a curve and heard a distant complaint of sirens. Then he started seeing small red objects hurled up in the distance like popcorn.

When he rounded the bend, he saw a big Coke truck jackknifed and tipped over. Kids were looting the spilled cans, shaking them up, popping them open and then hurling them at nothing in particular like fizzing hand grenades. One man was offloading cases into a panel van. A motorcycle cop was on the far side of the truck setting up flares. He had Cokes in all his pockets.

The windshield of the cab-over truck was smashed and the driver's head and one arm poked through. His face was white, with a lot of blood pooled on the pavement below, and it was pretty clear that the ambulance was too late.

Soon the kids noticed the cop and Coke cans started raining down around him. He shouted something and drew his pistol. Jack Liffey decided it was time to get out of there. He heard the first shot as he rounded the bend in a trot.

Cars were starting to back up and fill to U-turn across the shallow divider. A woman in a little Geo had a panicky look in her eyes. His Concord had a high center of gravity and got over without trouble, but an old Nissan Z was hung up on its differential and smoking one tire. A big white Land Cruiser caught bumpers with the Z and spun it off the divider. The spinning tire touched down and the Z lurched into a parked car.

Jack Liffey saw the last of the apocalyptic outbreak in his mirror and then he turned off. He wanted to be away before it all went nuclear.

Fifteen minutes later he found L.A. State, a clot of concrete bunkers up a hillside. He parked in front of a shingled bungalow with huge concrete praying hands on the front lawn.

A long flight of piss-smelling concrete steps led up to the campus. He found Social Sciences and then the right room number. A card by the door had three names pencilled in and various lists of hours, most of them crossed out. One of the names was Connie Beltran. News articles in Spanish and Gary Larson cartoons were taped to the wall.

"Xavier Gallegos?"

The man nodded. "Liffey?"

Gallegos sat at the first of the three desks in the deep narrow office, a handsome man in his thirties with fly-away dark hair. An anxious-looking student sat at the back desk trying to make himself so small he would be invisible.

Gallegos closed a book over a sheet of notes. "Let's get a coffee." He didn't invite the other man.

Outside he stopped with one hand on a high glassed railing that kept suicidal graduate students from hurling themselves over. "I hope you won't find it terribly hostile if I ask for some identification."

Jack Liffey showed him a driver's licence, and his simplest business card.

"I had a bad experience with a couple of guys this morning." He described the Cowboy and his pal. "I've run into assholes like them, enforcers for the big ranchers."

"Where was that?"

"Colorado. You think *Milagro Beanfield War* was just a book, don't you? I come from Chama, a place just like Chamisaville, and everything was just like that damn book. Everybody was named Archuleta and they were all a bit crazy in a nice way and the rich *gabachos* thought they owned the world."

"What did these guys want?"

"They went through Connie's desk. I knew better than to try to stop them. I might have objected if they'd found anything. I'm not sure. Maybe I would have."

"They didn't find anything?"

"She never left much there, there were always too many T.A.s and R.A.s using the office to leave anything that mattered. Why don't you buy me a coffee?"

He led across a walkway to an antiseptic snackbar with highly suspect coffee from a Kona machine. They took their tray outside to a plastic table.

"On the phone, you said you were her friend."

Xavier Gallegos just let that lay between them.

"You seem a little shy about her name."

"Mr. Liffey, I'm married. Connie and me were colleagues, we talked about Kevin Starr's books and the egregious Father Serra and Southwest social history. We both T.A.'ed in 150, a big non-major course called Missions to Orange Groves. We had lunch together a lot. My wife wouldn't understand this relationship at all so I don't want it on TV, if that's all right with you."

"She probably talked to you about the Cahuenga Neighborhood Organization and the election campaign."

"Of course. I helped her write some of the materials. A bunch of naive activists and do-goods, but. . . ."

"But what?"

He waited as a gaggle of young girls in white T-shirts wandered past talking earnestly. They looked like they were in junior high.

"Every once in a while do-goods do some good, but this one was pretty hard to call. Nothing was what it seemed. Slow Growth meant Mexicans Go Home. And Brown Power ended up meaning Slumlords 'R' Us. On balance it's hard to tell what was the best thing to do. Connie saw all that, I tell you she was a very bright lady, but she had a really long-term perspective. She said it was necessary to get some Latinos elected, even if the first batch were scumbags."

"So when did her focus on the neighborhood organization start changing?"

Gallegos looked a little surprised. "How did you know?"

"Why don't you tell me."

"I don't know very much. She told me somebody came to her with inside information, wheels within wheels. She said she wasn't ready to talk about it with me. Naturally that got me curious."

A red frisbee came over the railing. Gallegos reached out casually, caught it and tossed it back. "Waycool, thanks, dude," drifted up out of the steep void.

"Tell me about your curiosity."

"All I got out of her was it had to do with the Samson building. Everybody knows the L.A. powers that be were once talking about making the place a music center and shopping mall, but I'm sure they dumped that idea long ago. It never made much sense, seven miles from downtown. It'd be like putting the New York opera in Jersey City."

"She never told you anything more?"

He was silent for a moment. "That was right before she disappeared."

"Did your visitors say anything?"

He shook his head. "I don't know anything else."

"But what do you think?"

"I think I'm glad I don't know anything else. I don't think you're big enough to handle it, either."

"Handle what? You must have a guess."

He just shook his head again. Liffey could get no more, and as Gallegos bused the cups into a plastic tub and walked away, one thing was clear. Gallegos and Beltran had been lovers, and the man knew something that was scaring him to death. He was still working himself down through the fear.

• • •

BACK home, he did not know whether he was happy or unhappy and he thought about the pleasures of a good jolt of unblended scotch, which would have done either way. In an earlier lifetime. There were nine pages of long distance telephone calls from the opera society and he sat down at the kitchen table with a pencil and started making marks. He came up with 47 calls to New York, 30 to San Francisco, 22 to Houston, a scattering through the Midwest, a dozen to Amsterdam, 11 to London and 11 to Las Vegas. He looked at the call times and noticed that the Vegas ones were all late at night and figured somebody in the society worked late to talk to his bookie. Most of the cities were logical for opera lovers to call, but . . . Houston. Why Houston? Of course there were probably a lot of guys who dressed like the Cowboy in Houston.

There were only two different numbers in Houston and he jotted them down. In the morning he would try them or have Chris Johnson find out who they were.

The doorbell rang and gave him a chill. He pictured the Cowboy waiting on the step carrying some medieval torture device under his arm. He didn't have a peephole, but he was damned if he'd let them spook him and he swung the door hard and almost dragged her in. Marlena Cruz stood there in a tweed coat, which she opened sheepishly to show a sheer black nightie that barely got to her hips. Her large dark nipples showed clearly in the porchlight. She looked great.

"God, I didn't know how much I missed it, Jack. Am I welcome?"

"Is a bear Catholic? Does the Pope shit in the woods?"

9

DOING A GOOD JOB ON THE PARTS ONLY GOD COULD SEE

HE WOKE FOR THE SECOND TIME JANGLED BY A HUSTLE-
bustle dream. Marlena had awakened him the first time
dressing in the dark. He'd offered her coffee but she told
him to stay put. Sleepy and tender, he remembered kissing her musky thigh as she tugged into her nylons.

Now gray light leaked in and he had the feeling there
were a whole lot of better places to wake up, if he could
only find them. The condo with its white plaster walls
and aluminum windows had about as much personality
as a rental car. He heard the newspaper hit his front door.

He made coffee, read the paper with his feet up and
allowed himself to waste fifteen minutes doing the cross-
word. He was sure Mike Lewis wouldn't be up much
before eight.

He took Venice Boulevard and then turned up Al-
varado to avoid the freeway and came into Pasadena
from the back side. Lewis rented a decaying old craftsman on the slopes of the Arroyo with his Irish wife
Siobhann. She had some job with the city government
which was the reason they'd be up as early as eight.
Most of white collar L.A. started on Hollywood hours,

which meant nine-thirty or later, but the bureaucrats still gave a nod to their working class constituents.

Siobhann was just climbing into her rusty little Saab when he drove up, all feisty talkative ninety-eight pounds of her.

"Is that Jack? For sure it is. What are you doing here so early?"

"Hi, S. Do you mean what am I doing *here* so early, or what am I doing here *so early?* Is himself awake?"

She nodded. "You left a wonderful sweet on his plate. He was up half the night poring over your papers. You know how he loves going down a burrow of crooked politics like a ferret and coming up with the rotten meat in his teeth."

"I think you're mixing metaphors."

"Verbal extravagance is in the genes. Come for dinner some day, Jack. We miss you since we moved out here."

"I will."

It was an old two-cycle Saab, odd as a cockroach, and it farted away down the twisting street, sun through the big live oaks dot-dashing off the rusting chrome. Siobhann and Kathleen, his second-generation Irish ex-wife, were still friends. Unlike most divorces they hadn't really found they had to choose up their friends.

Lewis looked bleary, sitting at the Formica kitchen table with the paper, a store-bought powdered sugar doughnut and a huge mug of coffee.

"Morning," Jack Liffey said.

"If it is and I doubt it."

Something perky, maybe Mozart, was playing softly in the other room.

"I thought you'd get a kick out of those papers."

"Man, even if you specialize in turning over flat rocks, those are some damned entertaining memos. Can

I keep them for a while?" He took out a stick of cinnamon gum and offered, the only grown-up Jack Liffey had ever known who chewed gum.

"I wouldn't say no to some coffee."

"Help yourself, and then follow me."

They regrouped in the living room, which had little piles of papers scattered around with label cards like MANGAN and SLOW GROWTH on the stacks. The furniture was all late thrift store, and the only thing they'd put up on the walls was an old poster for the IRA hunger strikers. Lewis was probably the only human being on earth who had once lived in Northern Ireland by choice. He said he'd found it fascinating.

"There's a lot of stuff here that's no use to you but I can do a great article on the Cahuenga election and the aftermath."

"Can you tell where it came from?"

"More than one source. There's rather a lot from an old commission on the rubber factory. You know, traditionally, if you want something done in this city you set up a commission of businessmen. I think some of it's from the election committee and some from the group that Ms. Beltran's people were opposing. Some weird stuff is from a source I haven't identified. It's a lot of memos in a self-conscious kind of code. 'The shipment of wood is overdue at the rodeo'—things like that. It's been culled down before you got it, probably to some common theme, but I can't identify it."

Liffey idly peered at a pile labelled STRING BASS. "Was there anything to kill for?"

"Hell, people in this town will kill you for your pocket change. There's some material that's damned odd, I'll tell you that for free. Look at this."

He handed Liffey a memo from someone named Robert Forrest at the County Redevelopment Agency. A green Post-it, probably Lewis', marked a passage half-way through.

Arneson and Villalobos insisted that our plans for the "opera house" are still too premature for us to initiate an approach to the brown parties.

"Interesting," Jack Liffey said neutrally.

"What the hell are those quotation marks doing?"

"There *are* people who don't know about irony. How many times have you seen 'fresh fish' on a menu?" Liffey made the marks in the air with his fingers, like a quieter Victor Borge.

"These here quotes are working overtime. And who *are* the brown parties? Look here."

He folded out a big architectural drawing. It appeared to be a floor plan of a portion of the rubber factory, redesigned. The inset at the bottom where the information would have been was blacked out. "It doesn't look much like an opera house to me. This might be a little stage, but they haven't left much room for the flies and wings. And look at all the open space. It's the world's largest theater lobby."

"I don't know, Mike. This is like practicing archaeology on a single pot. Maybe this is a stage of construction, or it's meant for a department store in the same complex. It's too easy to find mystery."

"That's the fun of it. Give me some more time with the stuff. I'm an alchemist." He made a European gesture, kissing the clasped tips of his fingers in appreciation. "I am not without resources myself."

"Don't become the man who knew too much. There's a couple of nasty characters kicking around." He described the Cowboy and his pal.

"This just gets better and better."

On the way down through the arroyo, Jack Liffey was forced to stop behind three cars and a little backhoe that blocked the road. A rivulet of water meandered down the asphalt and under the car just ahead of him, where it turned abruptly and trickled off the pavement out of sight. As he watched, the flow quickened until it was a dark sheet creeping under his own car.

A car honked in annoyance. A workman in a silver hardhat waved his arm dismissively and the backhoe readjusted its position. Then things began to happen fast. The water gushed suddenly, like a tap turned on. Three workmen scrambled away from the backhoe with a look of panic and Liffey felt a rumble in the ground. A big scallop of the road broke away and disappeared from sight with a loud gulp that freed a plume of clear clean water. The backhoe began to lean, the driver abandoned ship as someone shouted, and the backhoe, too, vanished over the side with another big bite of the road. He noticed he was holding his breath and he made himself exhale.

There were no cars behind him and he backed away fast, followed immediately by a black Camaro. The last thing he saw was a big orange VW bus with a camper top begin to teeter. He pulled off into a driveway and the Camaro roared past in reverse. When he got headed the right way, he stopped and got out to look down below. Dirt and big lozenges of asphalt had filled up a back yard, covering half of a swimming pool as the stream of water played over a two-story frame house. The backhoe had landed upside down through the garage, and a bewildered-looking woman with a broom was staring up the hill at the VW that lay on its side, caught on some snag half way down. It didn't look like anyone had been hurt yet, but the day was young.

He stopped at a doughnut shop as the memory of

Lewis' powdered sugar doughnut stirred in him and
pointed to a plain cake doughnut. The Asian counterman
gave it to him in a piece of tissue. A stringy white
woman and black man sat at a corner table arguing
softly. They were unkempt and looked as if they'd slept
in a field. One of the latest ploys for panhandling spare
change was to act as unofficial doorman to a doughnut
shop.

Liffey sat in a red plastic chair fixed to the floor and
wondered why he was chasing down this scandal. Nothing he did would bring back Consuela Beltran. He was
a child-finder not a detective, and he felt awkward and
exposed, the way he had come to feel all of a sudden
during Tet, knowing that he was utterly vulnerable and
a bullet already in flight probably had his name on it. It
was a way you felt when you no longer believed in your
special place in the universe, or your fine-tuned instinct,
and all you had left was luck. The kind of luck that could
plunge over a cliff in the blink of an eye and end up
nose-first through a garage.

Why was he pressing his luck? He inventoried where
his pistols were at that moment—the Dreyse was back
with Marlena and the Ballester-Molina was in his bed-
side table—and he wished he had one of them in the
glove compartment. Somebody had killed Consuela Beltran and somebody else had delivered a packet of dangerous research to him, and two men had threatened his
life if he used the research. He was over the flush of
anger that had launched him on the crusade, and he had
trouble coming up with something else. Pride was in
there somewhere, he guessed, and a pigheaded kind of
indignation. And maybe he was doing it for the boy.

He wanted to see the faxes from the opera society.
Liffey tossed out the last third of the stale doughnut, and
the homeless man leapt up to hold the door for him, but

he was too late and didn't get anything for his efforts.

Chris Johnson was pottering in his garage-workshop where he was rebuilding an old sofa. The fabric was stripped off to reveal a crude-looking wood frame and a flimsy spring platform. It had started as Dot's hobby, but now it was his.

"With the cloth off it looks like a drowned cat," Jack Liffey said, regretting the simile immediately. Or a drowned woman.

"Even the good ones are marginal. This should have been hardwood, but it's cheap pine."

"Are they all as bad?"

"Pretty much. Only the Amish cared enough to do a good job on the parts only God could see. But they never made stuffed furniture."

"That's probably what happens to you when you give up fucking. Discomfort becomes a kind of esthetic."

Johnson smiled evenly. "Every discomfort makes you stronger. You should sit in a jail cell for a while. Everything that doesn't break you, concentrates your energy."

"Sorry, I forgot you were a jail-bird. I'll leave you all that manly conceit, thanks."

"This is the one you want." He offered a sheet of paper from his breast pocket. "The rest of the faxes were about buying costumes for Egyptian slave girls or scheduling performers or escrow papers for some guy who was buying his house on company time."

Liffey flattened out the paper on the work bench. It was outgoing to some vice president of the National Tobacco Company in Raleigh.

Dave, you're misinterpreting the thrust of our proposal. We would see that you buy the building for the figure you mentioned, outright. It's a sale-leaseback-

*buyback. It's a listed building, official county landmark,
so the Title applies and you get tax credits for what you
pay us, for preservation of historic landmarks. Ask your
bean counters. You could extend that easily enough to
much of your Western operations, but that's up to you.
We would lease it back year by year and then at the end
of 25 years buy it back out of bonds with a balloon
payment. You're out nothing at all really and you can
leverage the tax breaks so the feds and the state end up
paying at both ends. And you get the corporate image
massage, your name up in marble in the lobby and on
the programs. How long would it take to absorb the up-
front cost with the tax credits? You get paid back twice
over, at the worst. Have your people think it over. Don.*

Jack Liffey read it three times. "Let me get this
straight. A tobacco company back east buys an opera
house in L.A. and puts its name on it. Because the building is a landmark, they can count their cost as some sort
of charitable contribution to the people of the nation and
take it off their taxes."

"Bravo," Chris Johnson said. "In addition to which,
the city spends twenty-five years of lease fees paying
them back the money they already wrote off their taxes,
and then the city pays them again in a lump sum with
bonds our grandchildren pay for."

"Is this legal?"

"Legal-schmegal. The real corruption is always the
stuff that's built-in. It's all a bit academic, though, if
there's no opera house." He squatted down to sight
along the timber on the back of the sofa. "Warped beyond hope."

"Tell you what," Jack Liffey said, fascinated by the
naked audacity of the deal. "My Concord is a genuine
landmark, not made any more. You give me a thousand

bucks for it, and I'll bet you get a great big tax break for preserving Americana. I'll lease it back for ten bucks a month and then my grandchildren will pay you millions, millions. Sounds good to me.''

''But there's no opera house, Jack. It's just a rumor.''

''What seems to matter is that someone believes it.'' Peel the onion, he thought. ''But, really, do cigarette companies kill to keep their tax breaks? There's something else in all this.''

''You and I will never know for sure much of anything where big money is concerned. At least that's the conventional wisdom, the legend of our time. It's probably not true. The rich are probably even stupider and more confused than we are.''

''Speak for yourself. They couldn't be more confused than I am. All I've got going for me is pig-headedness.''

''Help me turn this over.''

They lifted the sofa carcass and set it upside down. Johnson began stripping the muslin off the bottom.

''I'd like to look through the other faxes.''

''I didn't print them. Okay, I'm tired of the sofa.'' He took Liffey back into the house and fired up one of the terminals.

Jack Liffey paged down the screen through fax after fax for the next 45 minutes. As Johnson had suggested, they didn't twang his curiosity much. Incoming were ticket orders, wheedling scheduling queries from visiting sopranos, memos requesting more details about costumes and business purchases, contentious demands by someone named Witold Mochnacki for small changes in a musical score, sketches of hyper-modern scenery for some new opera, and one request for escrow papers. Outgoing there were lease orders for 30 British police uniforms, an order to Germany for an HO scale toy train, pages of music, one lyric sheet, sketches of the same hyper-modern scenery with heavy black lines suggesting changes, and one set of escrow papers.

And then he found it, so short it stood out like a zebra in Pershing Square. *We'd best tell the N that we shall better any offer Houston makes for T.* It was a month old. The recipient was in New York, but the name was illegible. The sender was W.O. in the opera society here, and the syntax was British.

Could "the N" be anything but the Netherlands? And T was ter Braak. Houston again. Guys who dressed like cowboys came from Houston. Had they been in a bidding war for the impresario? Did opera societies bump each other off to get new bankable stars?

"Do you think somebody would kill to see an opera?" Liffey said.

"Only if he really wanted to," Johnson said.

HE GOT A WOMAN ON THE PHONE WHO SPOKE ONLY SPAN-
ish. It wasn't Senora Schuler, and it took her a long time
to comprehend his pronunciation of ''Tony, *por favor.*''

''Is this Tony?''

''Yeah.''

''This is Jack Liffey. Don't you ever go to school?''

''Abuela says I can stay off another day.''

''Did you find out anything about that car?''

''My homies seen it, man. Just like you said, all
blacked out. They seen it a lot in front of a place on
Heliotrope. Around four o'clock when men get off and
get a couple beers.''

''What's the name of the place?''

''I don't know. I gotta show you.''

''Describe it.''

''I gotta show you.''

He guessed the boy had his own agenda working.
Maybe he wanted to see what would happen when Liffey caught up with them, or he just wanted to ride
around in a detective's car. All Chicano kids wanted to
be seen in a beat-up '79 Concord.

"Will you be home if I come by at three-thirty?"

"Yeah, sure."

"If you see the car stay away from it."

"Sure. We see you Mr. Liffey."

We? he wondered. He looked around Johnson's computer room, all the beige on beige machines, heard techno music looping softly on a CD in another room, heard Johnson whistling to himself, and picked up the coffee cup that said *Total Quality Management means jobs*. The moment seemed so clean and exact. What did that mean? Was he about to experience something momentous? Or was there just a pocket of brain cells dedicated to alertness that was misfiring randomly?

"Got any death rayguns?" he called out.

Johnson peered in with a soldering iron in his hand.

"I could probably rig a laser to burn through someone, but you'd have to shoot him first to get him to stand still."

"That's too bad. I have a feeling I'm going to need an edge."

HE called the answering machine he'd got going again from the mess in his office and got three messages.

"Jack, I was hoping I didn't have to make this call. You're two payments behind now. It'll break Maeve's heart if I cut you off completely, but my lawyer says I can't let you see her at all until you catch up. I'm sorry. You know how lawyers are."

Blame the lawyer. It was like Kathy to find some roundabout way of softening the rough edges, not altogether a bad trait. It just left you punching air once in a while. Not for the first time, he thought of his marriage as a hat that had blown off while he was looking out over a canyon. He'd made a grab for it at the time, but then it was just gone, dwindling out of sight, leaving a bit of hat feel round his forehead but even that fading fast. It was the kind of thing that could still make you feel guilty about being broke, though.

"Jack, Mike. I think you might consider Houston, the city of no one's dreams. You know, the home of the Houston Ship Channel—the world's longest flammable body of water. There's some damn strange stuff I found about money passing that way. I'm still working on it."

Houston again. Opera societies didn't wage war. It was just too crazy.

"This is Arturo Castro, Jr. Call me when you're free."

Art*uro*. He called, but Castro was out. Liffey wondered if he'd found out anything more about the cowboy and his pal. He'd like any margin he could get.

THE Southern California Opera Society was up in the Bradbury Building where they did all the advertising shoots with the slim models in weird dresses posed arrogantly in front of the wrought iron elevator cages. There was a light well down the middle of the building, surrounded by open walks and gingerbread railings on every floor, like something from New Orleans, but a lot of the decorative wall tiles had fallen out and been replaced with plain tiles. The marble floor was worn and scarred, too.

Inside the opera society's glass doors, however, all was well. Pastels, Berber carpet, a hypermodern reception desk and a hypermodern receptionist with spiked blond hair and a big blue ice diamond.

"I must have turned left at Vegas," he said.

"Huh?"

"Nothing. I'm here to see Richard Cheuse. Did I pronounce it right?"

"Rhymes with juice. Who can I say you are?"

"Jack Liffey. Rhymes with spiffy."

She closed one eye, as if trying to decide if he was making fun of her.

"It's okay. I'm Irish. We sing ballads instead of opera."

She fiddled with her intercom. "Dick, I've got a Mr. Spiffy to see you."

A balding little man came from somewhere in the interior. "Mr. Spiffy, did you call me earlier?"

Liffey nodded. He didn't bother correcting him.

"Come."

The top of the man's head was iridescent under the hall lights, like an oil slick, but the rest of him was a West Hollywood entrepreneur, a suit in one of those Armani beiges and shoes that even Jack Liffey could tell were worth any three pairs of his own. He walked with a stiff little roll as if his muscles were ready for anything.

The office was dim, almost dark. "Light crushes things," he offered. "I like the quiet and I like the cool." His eyes wouldn't stay in one place. They roved, as if hunting out the danger that lurked somewhere.

"You wanted to talk to me about what?"

On the phone Liffey had said it was about some remaining real estate investments in Cahuenga. He didn't have much leverage, but Senora Beltran's sheaf of papers had given him that much.

"A woman was murdered in Cahuenga." Jack Liffey sat in an uncomfortable violet sling chair. "Perhaps you read about it."

"I don't really keep up with current events in that part of town."

"She was in an organization that was opposed to the opera society buying up Samson Rubber."

"That's ancient history. The building is a marvelous

piece of vernacular architecture, but hardly suitable for an opera house." There was a soft thumping sound in the wall, probably just the emanations of an old high-rise, but Cheuse's eyes snapped fiercely to the spot on the wall where the sound might have spawned.

"She also came into possession of a lot of papers from your files."

"Ah." He didn't go on, but the wall had lost its fascination.

"Do I make you jumpy, Mr. Cheuse?"

He shook his head, and Liffey had an inspiration. "What was your MOS?"

The searchlight of his eyes passed back to Liffey. "I was a Ranger, Third Special Forces Group"—he offered a fleeting chilly smile—"a fighting soldier from the sky. *Air*borne. I had *enthusiasm* for the mission, I got *with* the program." His fingers drummed the desk. "You know what I remember most, I remember walking through a village, all the kids lined up, going huh-lo, huh-lo, very soft and spooky, like doves."

"I remember being scared."

"Oh, yes, and *that*."

"I'm just an E-4 tech, but this woman and her son meant something to me. Do you have any idea what's going on in Cahuenga? And why you donated so much money to Slow Growth?"

It had been his biggest card and it didn't seem to be working. Cheuse rocked back comfortably. "I presume it was because we would have benefited. Slow Growth wanted an arts complex east of the river. Your friend was probably associated with the people who prefer slums to art. There are days when I do, too. But if I could make it a sequoia grove, I would prefer that to anything."

"You like trees."

"Don't you? Trees don't talk. I can never get enough quiet. You know, that fear—it wasn't just an extension of things you'd felt before. It was something so big and pure it was new, like stumbling onto love for the first time."

"I bet you haven't talked like that since the first weeks you got back."

"No. I wasn't a forest vet, but I could have been. I was on that path for a few days, hid out in a tent in Kings Canyon up by the Middle Fork, but it was too much melodrama. The great weapon against even that sort of pain is a sense of absurdity."

Liffey could hear, faintly, the crash of garbage cans in an alley, and then the beeping as a truck backed up. The sounds were distant, like listening to model railroad versions of real things. Perhaps that was what created the unreality of the whole interview.

"I don't want to disturb your equanimity," Liffey said. "I only have one more question. Why did you drop the plans for the opera house?"

He wasn't sure but it looked like disquiet in the man's eyes before they smoothed with calculation again, the surface of a pond ruffled as a rock passed through.

"The building wasn't suitable, and it was a county cultural monument so redoing it would have been too much bureaucratic trouble."

"It wasn't too much trouble for an expensive architectural firm to draw up plans. And a whole raft of bean counters were busy calculating the tax breaks."

The surface rippled again, and the spreading tremor of suspense passed out to the walls before dissipating as an extra flutter of ambient heat in the room.

"Mr. Liffey." He did seem to know the right name, after all. The words snapped all of a sudden like a twig in two hands. "You don't know enough to constitute a threat to anyone. You'd better go now."

DARK clouds were building up again to the north, but the sky was still sunny. For some reason there seemed to be a convocation of old Chevys along Slauson and he had to park a block from the Catholic Liberation house. It wasn't his day. His eye was drawn to a weedy lot by three skinny dogs nosing at something, and when he looked closer he saw it was the carcass of a fourth dog. The skin shifted and flexed where the dogs tore gingerly at the tissue, as if trying to avoid certain parts. It was not something you could watch. He didn't know dogs lacked the elementary civility to avoid eating their own kind. They were as bad as people after all.

Eleanor Ong was gone on a mission of mercy, some worker laid off from a battery plant on the east side who was succumbing to lead poisoning. The same kid in the Pendleton shirt was just as surly as ever.

"Have a swell day."

AS he drove up, he caught a glimpse of Senora Schuler out in back where Tony's weightlifting equipment was. She wore a housecoat, the first time he'd seen her untidy, and she wept uncontrollably, hitting the sides of her head with the palms of balled up fists. He had entered the zone of pain again.

The passage of Death was like one of those Midwest floods that tear open houses and leave unexpected things exposed to the world, unbearably intimate bedroom sets or broken toilets hanging in space. He didn't think she was a woman to show her emotions like this, and he held back and parked just out of sight to give her a minute to recover.

When he knocked, he heard a scuffle and the weeping

stopped abruptly. Senora Schuler peered out at him through the little grilled window in the door, then quickly opened. She took his sleeve with urgency and towed him through the house and out to the weightlifting bench. She pointed down at something that lay on a little plot of grass. It was a blued revolver. She must have found it in the house and hurled it out, like an offending rodent.

"Take away! You take!"

He bent down. It was an old Smith & Wesson .38 Chief's, with a three-inch barrel. About $250 at the swap meet. Blacks liked the fancy automatics, Glocks and Walthers, but Latinos wouldn't touch them and wanted only revolvers. Perhaps it was the tenuous historical thread to the Western six-shooter, or the reputation automatics had for jamming. He picked it up with a Kleenex and smelled it. It hadn't been fired and there was no smell of gun oil from a recent cleaning.

"Tony?" he said.

She nodded. "*La cama—debajo de* . . . the bed." She shuddered. "You take. Bad."

He slipped the pistol into his coat pocket. Obviously the boy was not there, and he was planning to make his apologies and go when she took his sleeve again and tugged him inside. She invited him into the kitchen and poured them both coffee, and they sat facing one another at the scarred table. So, she didn't mind visiting in the kitchen, after all.

She held her forehead in a hand and he could see her trying very hard to marshal her words. "My city. Hermosillo. Big city in Sonora." She shook her head, as if there were an ironic meaning in there somewhere. "Smart people go away. All smart people go away. Go Mexico, *distrito federal*. Go Nogales. Go *el Norte*, Chicago, California. Men go. Smart people go, we feel stupid. We stay. We no good.'' She made another face, as if shifting meaning again, so he could prepare to tack. ''Childs needs family. Childs needs uncles and ankles. Childs needs to hear names.''

She lit a cigarette, something Mexican from a dark blue pack, and it surprised him. He hadn't seen her smoke before. Her movements were very graceful and it was a pleasure to watch her wave out the match and set it gently in a shiny tin can.

''This not home. A little bit Mexico, but not home. It broken here. Big city. *Away* no good. Broken. City is mean, sadness, hungry, strangers.''

He could sense that there was something quite important struggling across the language barrier, and he knew a lot of it but not all of it and he was sorry once again that he didn't speak Spanish.

''City kill my Consuelita. Now my little little boy.'' She shook her head, her dark stiff hair hardly stirring. ''Is terrible.''

''I don't know what to do either,'' he said. ''We have to try to do what is right.''

He had thought her stolid and stalwart, another long-suffering earth-woman from the Third World, with Indian eyes and stocky frame, and he could see that was probably just another way he undervalued a culture that he couldn't contact. By all accounts her daughter had been brilliant. And in her, too, all along, something dark and shrewd and alert had moved beneath the surface.

Nothing happened in the kitchen for a while. She breathed. She sliced the burning tip off her cigarette against the lip of the can. She looked into his eyes and away. Eventually, he got up and left.

TONY slipped out of a yard and flagged him down at the corner.

"Man, she is mad today," Tony said.

Two friends were with him. Tony got into the front, and the other two slid to the opposite edges of the back seat, a window each, the four of them pressed into the far corners of the car. Tony introduced them but they wouldn't speak to the adult, didn't even meet his eyes. The chubby kid was called Nabo, and a mean-looking boy with a scar was Billy, if a thirteen-year-old boy could be said to be mean looking. All three wore khaki chinos and T-shirts with one sleeve rolled up to nothing.

Jack Liffey wanted to tell Tony that his grandmother was worried about him, but it was not something the boy would want to hear in front of his friends. Warriors left their womenfolk behind.

"Where to?"

"Up there." Tony waved ahead vaguely.

As he drove away, he wondered how to get through to the prematurely aging boys. It was the most difficult thing he knew. It was so much easier on the streets just to let things come, to improvise, simpler to be uncommunicative and just as hard as necessary.

All four of their heads swiveled abruptly to the same sight. It was a residential curbside, where a boy might have set up a lemonade stand in Liffey's youth, but here a boy of about fourteen held what appeared to be a comatose little girl across his arms, and a sandwich board around his neck said *Sister needs medisin*.

Liffey braked and all three of the boys reacted at once. "Don't stop!"

"Man, go on!"

"Keep going. Keep going!"

He stopped the car at the corner and looked at Tony, who was writhing in distress.

"He's *Setenta y uno*, O.G., man. They'll kill us here. For truly."

"He's asking for help."

"Man, you don't know nothing here. Maybe it's a trick, maybe a initiation, maybe he hurted her himself. They're bad *vatos*."

Liffey got out and walked back toward the boy. "Son, what's the problem?"

Fierce black eyes met his own. "Fuck off and die, cop."

"I'm not a cop. Do you need help? Let me see the little girl."

The boy swiveled her away, as if Liffey's touch would soil her, and then he fled across the lawn.

"*Cuidadito! Jura!*"

He watched the boy disappear between two cottages and then headed back disconsolately toward his car, the three moon faces in the windows watching him. At least, he thought, the twentieth century was winding down.

"You were right. You want to tell me where I'm going?"

"*Nachito's Billiares*. On Atlantic."

It was a run-down brick building with the tell-tale row of bolted metal plates high up under the architrave signifying an earthquake refurbishing. An old neon sign had once said Stan's Billiards, but it was rusting away and the new name was painted crudely on the window. There were also stickers saying "No Grapes." A dirt lot beside the building held several battered cars. There was no BMW.

"Okay. Go that way."

They directed him up a side street, then past an odd mini-mall that had been built far back from the street. Donuts, a laundromat, and *Video de Sonora*. But there was no BMW there either, nor in the alley behind.

"Maybe tomorrow," Liffey said.

"There's another place we seen it."

He followed their directions to a small office building, built of heavy concrete rectangles like exposed
bones, brutality as a kind of style. It belonged on the
West Side not here, but then he noticed that it was inhabited by accountants and lawyers. There were three
BMWs in the lot, two silver and one black, but not an
M3.

In a far corner there was a strange habitation. Trash
had been rolled and wadded into big tubes and then
banded with string. The coils had been built up into an
igloo just big enough for a human occupant. A fantastically tattered old woman squatted beside her home, one
hand protectively on a Ralphs shopping cart filled with
more building material. She seemed to be waiting for a
renewal of energy.

Just as he was about to pull out one end of the lot,
the M3 glided in the other, as blank-eyed as a bird of
prey. It gave a little throaty show-off spurt of speed and
then swung around and parked on a red curb near the
door. The first thing he checked was the plates. Very
recent California, with a number 3 ahead of the three
letters.

The boys had caught their breath, and there was no
need for anyone to point the car out. Jack Liffey backed
unobtrusively into a slot. The Cowboy got out of the
bird of prey, stuffed on his hat and said something into
the dark interior. His pal followed, arguing in a desultory
way. The Cowboy aimed his keyfob at the car, which
flashed its parking lights and then the two of them swag-
gered into the building.

Jack Liffey started his battered Concord and cruised
across the lot until he was only a few feet from the M3.
He popped his glove box and handed Tony a spray can
of white Rustoleum.

"Tag him."

Tony caught his eye.

"You can do it or I will."

Tony was out in a second, shaking the can until the ball rattled. The hiss of the spray cut through the distant hum of traffic as he squatted to hit the driver door expertly with a *placa* that looked like C60L in that Aztec writing that was all angles and reversed curves. The other two boys watched in awe. Tony crab-walked back, out of sight of the building, and tagged the rear fender. Liffey took up his post in front of the black car, looking calmly over it at the glass doors where they had gone in. The boy got bolder and hit the trunk, trailing a straight line of white around the car, and then he worked on the other door. In an office window a secretary looked on in horror, frozen to a standstill with a wad of papers in her hand.

"Get in the car."

Jack Liffey took out the boy's .38. He walked around the M3 and put a bullet into each tire, the shots crashing back to him off the building. The whooping alarm went off, with the headlights flashing and the horn honking insistently, and he put a shot through the windshield for good measure. He'd hoped it would shatter, but it just holed, leaving a neat ring and a few small cracks.

Then he waited at his purring Concord, staring back at the office building.

"Stay out of sight, gentlemen."

Finally the Cowboy came out in a rush but held up when he saw Liffey. They made eye contact, and then the Cowboy surveyed his car. The Cowboy's expression slowly warmed into a smile. Liffey felt his legs and arms tremble. He had a shot left and he could hurt someone in this frame of mind.

He got in and drove away.

"Jesus, Holy Mary, Mother of God," one of the boys in back repeated.

You only had the space you inhabited, and if you let someone take it away, it was gone forever.

11

IT'S POSSIBLE TO KNOW THINGS AND NOT BE COMPROMISED

HE STOPPED IN THE MIDDLE OF THE OLD DECO BRIDGE THAT spanned the L.A. River. The far bank was a moonscape of abandoned factories and smokeless stacks. A few birds flew against the bruised clouds. At a cement works, half a dozen conveyers rose steeply to gray hills like huge mantises tending their piles of dung.

He chose the exact middle where there would still be a little water in the mid-channel next summer and watched the .38 dwindle until the swift gray river swallowed it with hardly a sound. When they drained Mac-Arthur Park Lake to build the Red Line Metro station they found 1,800 handguns in the muck at the bottom, three generations of occluded carnage.

Back in the car he was fed up with warrior taciturnity. "What do you *vatos* want to do when you grow up?"

Now that they had seen the aging Anglo shoot up a car, they were willing to acknowledge him. In fact, he saw right away that they were still children underneath all the steel.

"I want to go to the Yucatan to catch parrots and sell."

It was the boy with the scar, Billy, speaking with an artless trust. Jack Liffey smiled. He'd expected more of a low-rent ambition, and he liked the idea of the parrot wrangler. He could see the boy, grown up and wearing tighter khakis from Banana Republic, leading an expedition off into the jungle with a big net at shoulder arms.

"Do you keep birds?"

The boy nodded solemnly. "I teach them to speak. *Chinga tu madre, esse.*"

Once Liffey laughed, the others did, too. They were still tough kids. "That parrot, he'd be a big hit in Beverly Hills. What do you want to do?"

Nabo screwed up his face in thought. "I want to work for an airline. I see the big airplanes all the time and I never been inside one. I want to fly in one."

"I have a feeling you will." Liffey turned to Tony, but he was not to be drawn so easily. His ambitions were more private and Liffey let them lie. He started the car. "I still don't know what I want to be when I grow up," Jack Liffey said. "But if some cowboy in a BMW wants to play, I'll play."

JACK Liffey knew he'd turned a corner. Up to that point in his life, he could always pretend he could go back and try another tack, maybe even find out what had gone wrong and fix it, but now the way back was harder to imagine. By taking up the Cowboy's challenge, he had marooned himself out at the exhausted edge of things.

A group of Latino kids played baseball in the street and he thought of the afternoon he'd hung on the wire fence for hours, watching little league games one after another, trying not to think of Viet Nam. Most of his friends had drawn magic lottery numbers but he had 37 and he didn't feel like doing a C.O. like Timmy Brice and he certainly wasn't going to tell a roomful of suspicious old farts that he was no C.O., but fuck *this* war, like Anthony Papadakis who was then doing eighteen months at a federal camp in Arizona. To tell the truth, the six weeks of Basic had been worse than the duty, sadistic gym coaches running his life. His duty hadn't been all that bad, monitoring air-conditioned instruments and watching green blips on screens. It was just that the tour had given him the first sense that the future was no longer provisional, and when the blips disappeared all of a sudden from the scope, he saw there was no way in hell to protect yourself from the future.

An unmarked cop car was parked in front of the boy's court. He wondered if the detectives had been sent to arrest the car vandals, but he doubted the Cowboy worked that way.

He stopped up the street and let the boys off. They'd seen the police, too, and they evaporated into the afternoon without a trace. Lieutenant Zuniga stood behind a screen door at the cottage next door to the Beltrans'. He had been talking to someone inside, but now he caught sight of the white Concord. The policeman pointed straight at him.

Jack Liffey got out and waited where he was. He wouldn't make it easy. The policeman lumbered down the walk and across the street like a tug heading for the next freighter. He stopped a few feet away as if sizing up where to moor.

"Is this where you pull my coat down and start punching my kidneys?"

To Liffey's surprise, the big policeman smiled, a tiny smile, almost against his will.

"Let's go for a walk."

Liffey was astonished, but he didn't show it. He followed along the sidewalk and ducked away from a pointy yucca that went for his eyes.

"You seem like an okay guy, I guess. As far as that goes."

"My mom thought so."

They went quiet as they passed a heavyset woman tending three small children on her lawn, and Liffey realized the two of them strolling down the Cahuenga back street must have stood out like giraffes in a supermarket. One child dropped a toy and started wailing. Far away there was a squeal of brakes and then a crash, but Lieutenant Zuniga didn't seem to notice.

"In a world of very bad things, okay guys can get hurt, whatever their moms think of them."

Jack Liffey felt a little shock along his spine. This wasn't a lovers' stroll after all. He wondered if the man had spoken to the Culver City police.

"You been in the Big Nam, I believe. Served your country."

"Something like that."

"You like your tour?"

"It had its moments."

"You weren't in combat, though, were you?"

"Only by accident a couple times."

"You know, more Hispanics died in the front lines than anybody. Per proportion and all."

"I heard something like that." They passed a little evangelical church with its name hand-lettered sloppily on a signboard. A building-fund thermometer was in the front, the red stuck down toward the bottom and fading. It didn't look like they were going to make it.

"Do you like the neighborhood?"

"Sure, it's great."

"They are lots of good ethical people living here who don't have a goddam clue about what really goes on in this town. They get up in the morning and get all the kids off to school and drive away in their fifteen-year-old junkers to their jobs in some bucket shop owned by some asshole from Brentwood. They work hard and mind their own business and when they come home the TV is always on to the noisy sitcoms from Argentina on the Spanish cable and they shop at the swap meet on Atlantic and never take a paper clip that doesn't belong to them. They *are* good people.''

"I wouldn't know about that."

"I know about it very much. I grew up here, when Hispanics still had to sit in back and the school counselors put us all in auto body shop.''

"You sound bitter."

"It gives you a certain perspective on good and evil."

"I see."

"No, you don't. You don't see shit.'' The policeman stopped in front of a weedy lot with a charred foundation. Something had burned down and never been rebuilt.

"Have it your way."

He nodded at the foundation. "Twenty years ago the L.A. SWAT team chased some Brown Berets into this house and shot them out. Didn't even have jurisdiction here, said it was hot pursuit or something. On the local TV live, just like the SLA. The place was so shot up it sat here empty for years until some crackheads torched it by accident.''

Jack Liffey was getting tired of veiled threats, if that was what they were. "Do all these object lessons have some kind of point?''

The policeman seemed to be chewing his cud. "I take it you've worked out that Senora Beltran discovered some things she wasn't supposed to know.''

"The thought occurred to me."

"I hope you don't take this wrong. Do you believe

that it's possible to know things and not be compromised?"

"Sure, why not?"

"I think I know what she discovered, but it doesn't do me any good at all and it wouldn't do you any good."

"Ah."

For the first time he noticed there was a derelict air raid siren on the block. A brown metal canister stuck up on a pole with the paint peeling off. It must have been twenty years since any of them had been tested, forlorn sentinals for a mad war that had never come. He remembered the Friday ten a.m. tests and then the surprise school drop drills, ducking your head between your knees and covering with your arms. He didn't think it had affected him much, but how could you tell? Maybe down deep.

"Is this advice or a threat?"

"Time changes things," the policeman said heavily. "Bad things go on and sometimes it's best if people get away with them. Then it's just fate or bad luck. You don't have to blame anyone, you don't have to answer why. The town has changed a lot and I had nothing to do with it. It'll go on changing and there's nothing we can do about it. Leave it alone."

Jack Liffey figured he already had enough people mad at him. "Well, then, I guess I better leave it alone."

THE early evening had an edge to it. He realized he couldn't go home or to his office. The Cowboy would get him either place sooner or later. It made him feel restless and angry, like wanting to hit someone. He parked six blocks from the Catholic Liberation house, up an alley in the deep shadows. The rear of the stucco bungalow where he parked had most of its windows broken and plywood over the back door, probably a crack house. They weren't all good hard-working citizens in Cahuenga. What had been a plank fence at the alley had fallen in and lay flat. He noticed flickering light in one of the windows only five feet away and couldn't resist.

Inside, a candle was guttering on a saucer, and the walls were fantastically covered with graffiti. A boy no more than sixteen was on his knees administering a syringe under the tongue of a girl with long stringy dirty hair. Where it wouldn't show, Jack Liffey thought. He shuddered and turned away just as the girl made a sound, like a cry of pleasure. He had a loathing of needles, something purely psychological about foreign objects penetrating his body, and he knew, no matter how low he sank, he would never be a drug addict, not if it had to be injected.

The Liberation youth in the Pendleton shirt was in the front room, moistening a mountain of envelopes ten at a time. He looked up at Jack Liffey resentfully, like a child suspecting a sibling of getting special privileges.

"I thought the Catholic Church had banks of eager women to do that," Jack Liffey said.

"This is the peewee league. She's praying in the Quiet Room." He nodded at the hall.

He found a door off the hall that said *The Quiet Room*, and decided that, all in all, the place was just a little too literal-minded for him. He knocked very softly twice and then went in. A few banks of folding chairs faced an alter with a small Jesus-laden crucifix where Eleanor Ong knelt with her arms dangling at her sides. She wore jeans that seemed to be painted on her hips and a navy blue leotard that made her look like an exercise video. He wished she'd go back to the gypsy skirts.

She made a shush gesture softly and returned to her praying, so he sat in the back row. There was very little to do besides look at the glistening stretchy fabric across her back and wonder how hard it would be to get off. He thought of Marlena, and once again wondered at how making love to one woman could make him want to touch another, and he didn't feel bad about it at all. He felt tenderness toward them both. It was also odd how just looking at a woman was such a physical pleasure, not even contemplating sex, just looking. That was something women would never understand.

For a moment his mind had drifted so much in the quiet that his consciousness went blank and he wondered with a jolt where he was. Maybe that was what meditation did to you. The room seemed more Quaker than Catholic. To be Catholic, he figured there ought to be incense, gold ornament, mumbo-jumbo.

"Amen," she said suddenly, and stood up. "Hi, Jack. You look upset today."

That worried him. "Do you really think there's some big consciousness up there listening to you?"

"You *are* angry."

"No, it's a question."

She shrugged. "I'm not sure. It'd be a hell of a thing to guess wrong, wouldn't it?"

He chuckled. "You know what Voltaire said on his deathbed, when they asked him if he was ready, *now*, to renounce the devil and all his works?"

She shook her head.

" 'This is a helluva time to be making new enemies.' "

It was her turn to smile. Even a tiny smile lit her up like a lighthouse.

"I think it's time we went to dinner," he said.

She considered for a moment. "It's not the impossible dream. I'll tell Jonathan."

"Be careful. He's already mooning around."

"He's very vulnerable right now. He left his family and dropped out of college and he's only been with us a few months."

"Why'd he do that?"

She hesitated. "At the beginning of his junior year his dad gave him a Lucien Picard watch, some gold thing that cost thousands."

"I can see how that would bust him up."

"He gave him the exact same watch for high school graduation."

Jack Liffey wondered what it would feel like to have a watch worth more than $29.95. And he wondered if he'd have gone and dropped out of Long Beach State if his father had given him the same Timex two years running, the one with the little window that showed the date. He didn't say any of this because he saw being a wiseass would probably upset Eleanor Ong and he didn't want her to cancel the dinner date.

She came back in a minute, with a pink sweater over the breathtaking leotard and a fringed leather shoulder bag. She certainly hadn't spent her life studying high fashion.

"You get to start fresh with me," he said. "Since you dropped the sister business, you can be Lenore, or Nora, or Ellie, or Lena. Take your pick."

"I think I'll stick with Eleanor for now. It's a poor thing but mine own."

"Actually," he said gently, "it's an ill-favored thing, but mine own."

"Really?"

"I have a very good memory. Is there a back door to the house? I'll explain later, but it would be a very good idea to go out the back."

She studied him for a moment. "You're serious."

"Oh, yeah."

She led him through the kitchen to an all-glass room that was full of sealed paper bags that looked like they contained second-hand clothing. The room was probably intolerable in summer. They shifted a dozen bags to get at the door, and she had to try out several keys on her giant plastic fob before finding the right one. He looked over her shoulder to read the fob: *Our Lady of the Plastic Rose.* He wondered where *that* came from.

He touched her back briefly going out the door and it felt great, lots of muscle tone. The alley was dark and something scurried away, driving her back against him for a second and that felt good, too. She hadn't recoiled from the touch.

"I knew a guy from New York," he said. "Wouldn't walk under palm trees any more after I told him they had rats in them. I guess he was afraid of them jumping down into his hair or maybe just a sort of rain of rat droppings."

"Is that true?"

"Sure. When I was a kid a lot of the palms along Paseo Del Mar had metal bands around to keep the rats from climbing. But, hell, rats have to live, too. The ecologists don't think of that a lot. Just the nice animals, like rabbits and dolphins."

"Rats bite children in the projects," she said.

"If they're as tough as Tony Beltran, good luck to the rats."

She was silent for a moment as they walked, splashing a little where water still stood in the alley. "What do you think will happen to him?"

"I think he's a pretty good kid, but a lot could go wrong. Every kid out there has a dozen pieces of heavy artillery aimed at him. I can see ten places in my youth where I could have gone bad. Anybody with spirit could. The temptation to steal something you really wanted, a few friends going out drinking and driving, a fight where I could have hurt somebody bad. Of course, there was the time things really did go wrong.''

''What was that?''

''I'm still trying to work it out.''

''Were you married?''

''Yeah. I've got a daughter named Maeve, she's nine. She's sweet. Looks a little like you. If I start thinking about all the things that could happen to her, I get sick to my stomach.''

''People adapt, even to the bad things if you raise them right.''

''Spoken like a nun.''

She was silent for a time. ''It wasn't all coddling. I've had my adapting, too, Mr. Liffey.''

''Mr. Liffey's my dad. I'm Jack.''

They were getting close to the car. ''Wait here.'' He didn't want her glancing into the crack house, but when he got to the car he noticed that the candle was out.

He caught her in the headlights and she looked like a blinded deer. He felt a desperate tenderness toward her, toward Maeve, toward Tony and his friends, toward everyone caught out in the rain of ratshit.

"**WHY** did we go out the back?'' she asked after the Thai waiter padded softly away.

''A couple guys have a feud with me. They know my car by now.''

''Does it have something to do with Connie's death?''

''I wish I knew. All I know is they pissed me off and then I pissed them off and they're not going to be kidding around any more.''

''Why did you?''

''It's a long story.''

"We have all night."

He tried to read that comment, but couldn't. Perhaps she just meant all evening. There was a lot of red in the room, from paper lanterns and posters of Bangkok and big red menus and the glow made her skin look absolutely magnificent. "I can stay polite only so long under pressure. It's like an itch. You know, bad manners can be a kind of freedom sometimes."

"I think I know what you mean."

"Fitting in got to be a chore for you, didn't it?"

"What do you mean?"

"The nun thing, the religion where people do what they're told."

She waited, looking at her nails as if deciphering a message written there, then she looked up as if she'd made a decision.

"You'd be surprised how much personality nuns have. Sometimes I think they get spoiled with it—the way the nun's life conspires to keep them infants. All the moral earnestness and caring for others without any real personal connection. They all stay younger than their age."

"You don't seem so much younger than your age. Oops. That's a trick question."

"Half the nuns I know were afraid to stop smiling. I think they felt like God's TV shows. If they ever stopped being nice, He'd switch them off. Cancel their season."

He laughed. "How did they ever let someone as pretty and headstrong as you take orders?"

"I can't be flattered, Jack. I'm too vain. Why did we go out the back?" she added doggedly.

"I don't think you'd believe me if I told you."

"Try me."

The waiter brought two huge beers and Jack Liffey waited as the man decanted a sampling very slowly into tilted glasses and then moved away soundlessly.

"I think the world can be a bit rougher than you know." He told her obliquely about the rattlesnake. "They wanted to scare me away from looking into Senora Beltran's killing. I scare pretty easily, but I also get angry. I have a kind of personal code about people getting up into my face. It's the only face I've got. This afternoon I got into their face."

He told her what he'd done, and describing it made it seem even crazier. It had seemed to make sense at the time.

"Why on earth did you do that?"

He sighed. "I'm not sure. I know those two are at the heart of this thing and I'd like to see who starts buzzing when the brick hits the beehive. Of course, I can't go home for a while."

She digested that as the seafood appetizers arrived.

"You're wrong," she said finally. "About my naivete, anyway. Remember, I was taught Original Sin. We start from the assumption that things are rotten."

"Yeah, well, a rotten time *out here* doesn't mean going to bed without your supper." He wasn't sure why he was being rough with her. "It means little girls get raped in the park and some men enjoy inflicting pain."

"I'll take that under advisement."

For the rest of the dinner, they talked about other things and they both loosened up. He did his best to turn on the charm and she was enlivened, smiling and laughing, touching his hand when he lit a cigarette for her with the candle in the red glass cup, and he thought he sensed a promise in her manner, but he was reluctant to think about it too much. His emotions were volatile enough already.

•   •   •

"So where are you going tonight?"

They were strolling along a residential street behind the restaurant, a little too shadowy for comfort. Far in the distance someone howled, perhaps in pain, and they both stopped to listen. All they could hear was wind and traffic, and a scattering of dogs, touching each other off like a long-distance conversation. She held his upper arm with both hands and his skin burned where she touched him.

"I can't very well say, Your place or mine."

"We don't usually entertain gentleman callers at Liberation House, but there aren't any rules."

"Is that a yes?"

"Jack, I'm a little afraid of you. You're really at loose ends, aren't you?"

"Yeah."

"I don't know if I'm strong enough."

"Don't kid yourself. You're more ragged than I am."

"That's the problem."

12

A KIND OF FAITH IN LIFE

THEY TIPTOED UP THE CREAKY WOOD STAIRCASE HOLDING
hands. The old wainscoting showed many generations of
paint, and fading posters pleaded leftish causes, *anos de
mujeres* and big doves hunting forlornly for peace. It
was not a hallway that had much use for irony.

"You'll be grounded for a month," he suggested, and
she shushed him.

Her door was at the end of the hall. The room was
far less tidy than he'd anticipated, more art studio than
bedroom. A big black and white charcoal sketch of a
Latino festival was on an easel, bustling with crinolines
and sombreros. On every surface and tented against the
walls there were other drawings, mostly of people, old
craggy faces, grinning children, workmen on building
sites. Out of the corner of his eye he saw her hide a
sketch discreetly behind some others.

"Art or therapy?" he asked. He went straight to the
one she'd sequestered and tugged it out against the pull
of her arm. It was of him, one leg of his pants hiked up,
sitting on the edge of the desk downstairs, as she must
have seen him. He thought he looked overbearing.
"From memory. That's remarkable."

"I have a little wine."

She wiggled the cork out of a half empty bottle of some sweet white wine and poured it into two juice glasses. She was very nervous, most of her brashness having stayed behind somewhere else.

"Do any of these date to your religious years?"

"I didn't realize my religious years had ended."

"They end tonight."

"You forget that I always have the option of confessing."

"Do you regret it already?"

She sat on the edge of the bed and took off her deck shoes, and he studied his portrait glumly. "We never see ourselves the way others do. The things that you think show don't, and all the things you want to hide show. I wish I could draw you."

"I have a better idea," she said. She tugged off her sweater with a cross-armed exercise in geometry and then worked on the leotard top in an unladylike way. It seemed to unsnap down in the crotch, under the buttons of her jeans. She peeled it off to reveal uptilted breasts and a world of freckles. "Of every fruit of the tree you may freely partake."

He figured he'd better nudge things forward before she fixated any further on being the Vestal sacrifice at his barbarian altar.

"Cheer up," he said. "It can actually be fun." He knelt to kiss her and found her grasping him hungrily.

For a while she grew more tense and then something in her switched off—or on—and she forgot that she had to worry it to death and began to work herself down into enjoyment.

"What a treat, Jack's penis," she said, holding him in her fist like a gear shift. She smiled grimly, but neither of them could get it inside her. They tried with him on top and then she tried to lower herself onto him, but he could see her wince and it put him off. A combination of nerves and disuse, he figured. The virgin state may have passed technically but the sanctuary was still reliably locked up.

"Things will loosen up," he said.

As if to compensate, some flood of sensations unloosed and she came unexpectedly to his touch.

"Zowie zowie," she said, like something from comic book onomatopoeia. "Now it's my turn." And she was all over him, trying to do everything at once.

Only when they were done, and lying damp and hot against one another, did she begin to worry about the others in the house again. "I don't know how to deal with this in the morning."

"I could leave very early."

"Maybe it would be best. But I want to sleep next to you. I've never actually woken up next to a man, opened my eyes to see hairy shoulders."

"They're not that hairy. Are you going to sketch me like this?"

"It's the way I grab onto things." Her fingers explored the shape of his face. They were silent for a time, wind whispering and insinuating at the window.

"Are you going to confess this?" he said after a while.

"Your engine is going all the time. There's no neutral, is there? I have this feeling you're always looking for something. Did something disappear from your life?"

"My wife and daughter."

"Ah, of course."

"Don't overweight it. Whatever went AWOL for me was long before that. They probably left because something was already wrong. I hear existential dread comes from a missing vitamin in the diet.''

''I doubt it,'' she said. ''There's a God-shaped hole in my life.'' She closed her eyes. ''I believed for so long and so fervently. When you first lose faith, you still believe there's something there to find again, very close by. Then after a while you can only hope there's something somewhere. In the end all you can do is cling to the *idea* of faith, like a secret lover.''

He kissed her cheek softly. ''You behave well,'' he said. ''That's what matters.''

AN onshore breeze had brought cloud like a low gray ceiling, and drizzle made the streets reflective and hissy. He had tiptoed out at five, and he watched the sunrise from a 24-hour Denny's, where he read every word of the morning *Times* until he could return the call to Art Castro. Castro finally got to work and summoned him to a meeting at a place called Cahuenga Concepts across the river on Firestone.

He kept looking out the corner of his eye for the black M3 as he crossed the concrete river, one of his wipers torn and leaving a blur. Then he realized that that car would probably be in the shop today. He wondered what they would be driving, or if they'd just track him down from an armored helicopter that fired missiles. Sooner or later, he would have to deal with them.

Castro was waiting in the lot in his misted-up Lexus. Jack Liffey rapped on the window, and it came down with an electric whir.

''Hi there, Art*uro*.''

''I been thinking about something,'' he said without preamble. ''You Catholic?''

''No.''

''I went to parochial school. You know what the nuns

used to say to the girls? Never eat ravioli on a date because it will make the boys think about pillows. Can you beat that?''

"I know a better class of nun," Jack Liffey said, thinking about Sister Mary Rose.

They went in together, a small lobby with glass cases where they had to wait while a beautiful black receptionist with beads in her hair checked on the phone. One display showed a Magic Golf Cleat that retracted into your shoe so it didn't mar the clubhouse floor. There was a self-inking date stamp, a teflon wok, a big plastic salad spinner that ran on batteries and a display of writing paper with *The Official . . . of the World Cup* printed on each sheet. Official what? he wondered.

"Mr. Pelopidas will be right out."

Art Castro made a point of walking around the room, studying the displays. The golf cleat display had a TV silently playing an 800 commercial, an extreme closeup of a shoe walking on wood.

"See how the rubber cup stays extended on a hard surface. It's really clever."

It might have been irony. Art Castro wasn't always easy to read.

"I try to remember everything I see," he said. "It takes time, but you never know when it will come in handy."

"I try to forget as much as possible," Liffey said. "I just hang onto skills."

"Always the tough guy."

A short stocky man looked in, his skin olive and his glistening black hair slicked back tight. "Gentlemen. Please come this way."

It was an odd office, the size of a basketball half court with four desks, one per wall, each facing inward as if the geographic center of the room contained something to be watched, but the center held only a work table and some lateral filing cabinets. A man in an old-fashioned vest pecked at a laptop at the north desk—Jack Liffey always liked to be oriented. Pelopidas headed for the east desk, which looked the best and biggest. A woman in a woolly two-piece was methodically Xeroxing from one pile into another near his desk.

"Sweetie, can you do that later?"

She seemed startled. "Sure, Mr. P." She tidied the two piles and sauntered out a door.

"Real nice ass," Pelopidas said. "We let the real estate people share our Xerox so we can look at their girl's ass."

"Understandable," Art Castro said. "If not politically correct." They sat facing him.

"Nobody gets pregnant looking, and when nookie goes out of style, we're all gonna be in deep doo-doo."

"Opera," Art Castro said.

"Yeah, something like that. Opera. You know, we was the first pioneers of the cable ad. You bring us your invention and we help produce it and then we set up a boiler room of telephone ladies somewhere and we start flogging ads to the little cable outfits in East Hogback. You pace yourself real careful and you can build up the cash to go to the bigger cables and bigger still until everybody in the country's dying to buy your no-battery flashlight. We provide a genuine service for the little guy, let him compete with Mr. GM and Mr. Ford."

One of the fluorescents buzzed annoyingly, but no one seemed to notice.

"Opera," Art Castro said.

"Sure, opera. We was setting up this boiler room not far from Houston a few months ago. God-forsaken place called Alvin. We like to grace these little towns where maybe a lot of housewives want some pin money, and they don't want an arm and a leg for coming in, answer the phones. So we go to rent a storefront and in the course of normal business we meet some real estate gentlemen of the cowboy hat persuasion. And later these guys come to us, because we got an L.A. operation, and ask us to help them out with some L.A. business.''

The north phone rang, and Pelopidas held up while the other man met his eyes and got some unspoken signal. The other man punched a button and the phone went silent.

''Thanks.''

Jack Liffey stared at this other man, his bald spot chalky, and a kind of slackening at the corner of his lips, like a sneer waiting to bloom. He was sure he'd seen him somewhere before.

''It seems they got a big place called the Petro-Center they're thinking of upgrading to an entertainment complex, bug out of the old offices that ain't doing so well since the oil business went eighty-six. All they gotta do is get this guy in Holland or somewhere to come over, give the go-ahead to be their maestro and the money'll just fall into their pockets. But this guy, it seems, some people in L.A. been sweet-talking him and he asks more and more money every time they ring up. Guy gets a swell head. He wants a better opera house every time they talk. First it's more seats and practice rooms, then some kind of red stone outside and jobs for his friends, and then he wants to hold them up for a place to live and a car.

''So they ask us to look into this end. They want to donate some money to folks that aren't too happy about taxpayer money building an opera house in L.A. Now, we can't give this money directly for a number of reasons, but some of the big winners are a Vietnamese family, got a lot of gold out of their country in 1972 and bought apartments in Cahuenga. They hate the Slow Growth people for their own reasons and it's the Slow Growth people who like to hear fat ladies sing. So we made a marriage and took a little commission, and the Phan Somethings passed some of the money on to the Cahuenga Neighborhood Organization and the rest is history. Slow Growth is out, the Opera House is out, but this ter Braak throws in a monkey wrench and comes to L.A. anyway. Must've liked the smog.'' He shrugged.

''Your friends in Houston weren't mad?'' Art Castro said.

''That's why I'm talking to you. Any trouble anybody can stir up out here, it's just fine with them. They figure somebody here owes them a freebie. May as well be you guys.''

It was all making less and less sense. If Pelopidas was right, his backers wanted to help the Neighborhood Organization, they didn't want to kill off its secretary.

''Your Houston pals, any of them drive a black BMW?'' Jack Liffey asked.

He shook his head. ''These are Cadillac kind of guys. You don't find a lot of foreign in Texas. These guys still wear the powder blue doubleknit suits with the piping over the tits.''

Castro questioned the man for another ten minutes but got nothing else useful.

''What do you make of that?'' Jack Liffey asked when they got outside.

''God knows. It matches what I heard from another source.''

''This is getting crazier by the minute.''

''So far all my sniffing around is for love, but. . . .''

''You don't want in this, Art. There's a couple guys out there want to whack somebody, and they're coming in low any minute. And nobody in this has got any money to speak of.''

''Why are you doing it?''

''My forebears were croppy Irish peasants, stuck with eating grass when the British exported all the food. It's left me with a bad temper.''

''Wire Paladin, San Francisco.''

''You got to protect the weak, Art. This country has turned on them.''

HE telephoned Mike Lewis and told him about the BMW and about Cahuenga Concepts.

''Art's such a wanker.''

''What do you mean?''

''There's a lot more onion. The Houston Opera Company didn't send a hit squad to L.A., trust me.''

''A Houston developer, not the opera society.''

''No way. Keep your head down and call me back later today. Keep out of sight.''

SO he did. He kidnapped Eleanor Ong and drove her up across the San Fernando Valley and then west toward what looked like a seam of light under the dark sky. She had been reluctant to go, full of her musts and mustn'ts, and then she had crumpled all at once and hugged his arm.

''The hell with duty. Just once, the hell with duty,'' she said.

They drove through a little rural town that looked like a snapshot of the 1930s and then he turned north through the hills, past a sign that warned them away from the condor sanctuary.

''I feel like a condor,'' she said. ''Some artifact of evolution. Some days I can't believe I was ever part of a monastic order.''

"Which days are those?"

"Most of them. I just don't have things figured out."
She seemed sad for some reason.

"I know," he said. "I don't have a clue any more,
either. But that's the way it's got to be. Any other way
is smug simple-mindedness."

She squirmed in the seat to study him. "You always
act like you've got things under control."

"That's the white male's burden. If we didn't act that
way, the world would fall apart. The thing to do with
your anxiety is to crank it all the way up to dread. It
tends to make you very polite and watchful on the surface."

"What *are* you talking about?"

He laughed. "Things are just too complicated. Let's
not go back."

"Let's not. We'll drive to the moon." She lay her
hand on his leg and the skin under his trousers burned.

For a moment he let himself imagine running off with
her, abandoning everything in L.A. to drive on north-
ward over the hills and let the road throw them up in
some Central Valley town like Tulare or Visalia where
they could start over with new names and new personalities.

He recalled his fantasy of the Canyon Country dog
ranch with Marlena and felt vaguely guilty, so he down-
sized the new daydream. He would sit in a glass booth
and sell gas at night as the trucks rumbled past, and she
would waitress in an all-night fly-blown EAT. They
would rent a motel by the week, and he would bang in
at dawn through an old wooden screen door and they
would make love on clammy sheets.

"I want you inside me," she said. "Really inside me
this time."

• • •

IT was surreal, as he knew it would be. Only an hour from L.A. and a postcard river meandered through a rolling valley, guarded by a scattering of live oaks. Past the graded trail there wasn't a single sign of civilization.

She looked around vaguely.

"That's the Sespe, the last free flowing river in Southern California. No concrete, no weirs, and it runs all year long."

The blue-gray river rippled over rocks at the foot of the hundred-foot cliff it had carved. From where they stood, the meanders stretched away until they broke up into dots and dashes of water glimpsed in the high grass.

"It's lovely."

He was disappointed that she didn't seem very impressed, as if he'd built her something that wasn't quite good enough. He turned the engine off and the wipers stopped half way so the view started going diffuse with mist.

"Have you ever known anyone who killed herself?" she asked.

"I show you a fabulous river and all you can think about is suicide?"

"I'm sorry. I just heard today. She was Catholic so it makes it worse."

"Not really," he said. "Dead is dead." He realized he was being unpleasant. "Was she a friend of yours?"

She nodded and rested her head against his shoulder.

"Best pals. She laicized a year ahead of me. A sweet girl from Michigan with really abusive parents, but I thought she turned out pretty good. Very earnest."

For a while there he had felt great, but nothing good ever lasts very long. "I didn't think it was possible to be more earnest than you."

She chose to ignore that. "It's amazing how attractive energy is, at least as long as its not mean-spirited. She glowed with it. She was interested in so many things, even if she never went very deep into any of them. I just don't understand it. I thought she was happy. I wonder if it can just sneak up on anybody, like cancer?''

He turned the key a notch and the wipers cycled down, clearing some of the view for a moment. He opened the side window, and realized it was actually not cold out at all. He could hear the splash of the river and a breeze in the trees and something else, a bustling ambience, just the *outdoorsness* of it all.

''I guess she ran out of beginnings,'' Eleanor Ong said. ''We used to talk about how we had lots of them, and we could start over and over if we wanted. Some days I can imagine that feeling just going away for good and you can't see anything new at all and then you've got to keep yourself running on, whatsit, just your momentum.''

Momentum wasn't so bad, he thought. What else was there? But he didn't want to talk about that.

''I'm not sure I like the way you look at things,'' she said. ''Everything disappears into a big black hole for you.''

''There's such a thing as a sense of honor,'' he said. ''I believe in that.''

She pulled away a few inches to look at him. ''Is that why you're helping with Connie Beltran?''

For an instant he had a feeling that whatever he found out about Consuela Beltran would clarify things for him. Up until that moment he had never consciously thought about it that way. Then the feeling fled, and he knew whatever he found out would do him no good at all. That was just a superstitious itch for order.

''Come on.''

He took her hand and they stepped out into a drizzle so light that it hardly dampened them. He plucked a plastic raincoat out of the back and handed it to her, but she ended up just carrying it balled up in her hand as they stepped carefully over the big slick rocks at the river's edge.

Willow switches bobbed back and forth on the far shore, and something leapt out of the water and then gulped back down before he could see it. She stumbled and he stiffened his arm to give her leverage. He was glad she was being quiet because he didn't want to hear any more about suicide or black holes.

The rocks gave way to sand and weeds, a band between river and cliff. Water beaded in her hair. He took the raincoat from her and spread it out on the shore, the plastic tenting up where weeds wouldn't smooth over. He held her and she kissed back. It was strange, feeling the cool damp between them. He wanted to chase away the sadness and he began to undress her very gently, folding her striped shirt and setting it on a big clump of white sage. She teetered and caught her balance as she stepped from foot to foot while he slid off her panties, leaving gooseflesh down her thighs. Then she started on him. She folded his clothing decorously, and she teased herself, revealing then covering then revealing his erect penis, until the self-consciousness went away in a laugh.

They lay on the raincoat and touched each other and licked the moisture off their bodies. He tried several ways to enter her, and when he managed it at last she hollered out, not in pleasure, but in a kind of relieved triumph. The sound echoed off the cliff and rolled away across the Sespe's flood plain. In the end she wept and clung to him and he found himself saying that he was falling in love, which was the simple truth.

On the way to an overpriced meal in Ojai, she returned to what he had been trying to drive away.

"Maybe you commit suicide when you finally decide that there's nothing left to figure out."

"Then being a detective is a kind of faith in life, isn't it?" he said.

13

ONE HEADLIGHT SEEMED TO BE OUT AND HE HEADED FOR A bright gas station in a townlet just off the highway. The road curved off between a pair of giant live oaks that stood like sentinels, and past the trees, what was left of the town looked like a few old teeth in a shattered denture.

"What happened?" she asked.

"The Northridge earthquake happened," he said. Most of the shops had migrated a quarter mile west into a row of prefabs that had become permanent and looked utterly dispiriting in their featureless blandness. A few old shops that remained were buttressed by wood braces.

"The earthquake do all this?" he said to the old man who waddled out of the gas station. Thermal underwear extended from his rolled up shirtsleeves, like a baseball player in late autumn.

"Town went to shit," he said nonchalantly. "But it ain't the only heartbreak."

"What do you mean?"

"Stable of horses burned up last week out at the flats." He was still coming slowly. "We had an Olympic hopeful in the shotput go down with a nerve disease. Then there's Bosnia.''

"You're a connoisseur of bad luck.''

"Just a realist.''

Jack Liffey pointed at the headlight and saw that the glass was broken. He must have picked up a rock, unless someone had shot it out. "I used to subscribe to the theory that expecting the worst kept you alert," Liffey said.

The old man took a screwdriver out of his back pocket and worked at the chrome rim. "Used to? You up and turn into an optimist?''

"I just could never figure out where the rounds were going to come from. Melancholy didn't help me much.''

"Too true.'' The old man worked out the remains of the bulb. "Let's see if we got your size.''

Catching sight of Eleanor Ong through the streaky windshield made him feel tender and weak inside, the way seeing his daughter did. How could you protect someone against all the bad luck? The plague even stalked a little backwater like this.

Her window was down an inch and he rested the tips of his fingers on the rounded top of the glass. She caressed his fingertips, the touch so electric he started getting an erection and had to readjust his trousers.

Love meant worrying about someone, he thought. Anxiety, suspicion of strangers, fear of the future. That's the way it worked. He took his hand away. How come people always ran toward it, then?

"It's gonna be kinda yellower, the new bulb.''

"I don't care what color it is.''

"Even in L.A. you'll have a hard time getting exact with this car. They haven't made no AMCs for fifteen years. Government only makes 'em stock parts for seven.''

"That was the problem with it," Jack Liffey said. "It lasted."

The old man tinkered and prodded and had to force the base of the bulb into the socket. "Car this old, I reckon you've seen some of your own bad luck."

"Just my share."

The old man straightened up and slapped rust off his hands, and Jack Liffey put the new bulb on the one credit card he hoped still had a little credit on it. He was not looking forward to taking Eleanor back home. "What's to do around here nights?"

"Not much since the ballet left town. The bar down the road there is all Mexes. They won't hurt you, but you may not feel *mucho bienvenido*."

The old man offered the carbons, and Liffey shook his head. He tore them in half and tucked them in the paper towel box on the side of a pump.

"All the luck in the world, mister."

"You, too."

Jack Liffey got in and headed reluctantly back toward L.A.

"I heard you two talking about bad luck. Are you bitter about your life?"

"Not really," he said. "The people who get bitter are the ones who think bad luck means something."

"How's that?"

"You just bought yourself a story." He grinned to himself. "My uncle had this door up into his attic made of frosted glass, this was in Michigan. I don't know why it was glass but it was. One day I saw a bit of a shadow on the glass and it moved and startled me, a little living shape, and I thought at first it was a mouse, but it kept making this tiny ticking sound on the glass. Tick-tick-tick. I went up the folding ladder and saw right away it was a robin. It had been up there a long time and it was pretty weak, but I still couldn't catch it to get it out of there.

"So I got my uncle and we chased it across the attic holding up bedsheets to corner it. I got it finally and that little lump in my sheet started to make its distress call, a high-pitched screeching so awful that you wanted to kill it right there, anything to stop it. I had to climb down and cross that house with this bird banging against my hands and screeching a mile a minute. Out on the back porch I tossed it up in the air. The bird fluttered up about ten feet and then took off for a vacant lot, but it didn't have much strength left and it was losing altitude all the way, still going like a tiny smoke alarm.

"It went straight in like a glider, and the instant that scared robin hit the weeds, I saw a big blur of black above it. It was a shiny old rook the size of a cat diving straight down on the robin. That scream went up a note, and then the rook was flying away with the robin in its beak. I never even knew rooks were meat eaters. Now that was one hard-luck robin, I'll grant you that, and saving it temporarily like that made me feel like some agent of doom, but here's the punch line. You'll never convince me there was some sort of pattern in that bird's bad luck, no numerology or fate or God's big plan. That robin just couldn't keep its mouth shut at the wrong time. Ten minutes later or ten minutes earlier the rook might have been off somewhere else. The robin might have dived in the weeds and found a nest of worms and fattened up so it lived to tell the tale. You can't get bitter about that. It's a crapshoot. If you're willing to take the good, you can't get angry about the bad."

"So, you're a stoic saint. I get it."

Telling the story, or her reaction to it, had left him vaguely unsatisfied. Nothing had been granted. She was still sending God get-well cards.

"Are you really happy being a detective?" she said after a time.

"I don't think of myself as a detective. I find lost kids."

"You're not looking for lost kids right now, though. Aren't you worried about the men after you?"

"I should be. Maybe I don't have enough imagination. Are you happy being a do-good?"

"It's close to what I used to do, what I was trained to do," she said. "Do-good." She toyed with the words, as if trying to decide whether to protest.

"That's not an answer."

"I'm in some kind of transition, Jack. I can't get a focus. Things seem too complicated. Some days little things pester me and some days I feel fine with what I'm doing."

They were funneling down a dead straight blackness between vast groves of orange trees, like a deep velvet version of night. It was hypnotic and eerie, the kind of road where the county put up signs telling you to run with your lights on during the day.

"You know the word *noise*? In engineering? It means too much data, you're getting data you didn't expect mixed in with the stuff you did expect. You're getting noise in your life. You thought all you had to do was deny yourself and love God and do your duty and you'd be satisfied forever and ever. Then this biological alarm clock started buzzing and telling you, What's in it for me?"

"That's too schematic, but there's some truth in it."

"I'll bet nobody's ever made much of an effort to know you."

"What do you mean?"

"All you nuns, you probably take each other for granted, sitting around your big wood tables. You haven't been married, and you probably didn't get really serious with anybody before you took the vows, or you wouldn't have taken the vows. And at the Liberation House in Cahuenga you look like you're the den mother, watching over everyone else. I'm just guessing. You get so flattered when somebody looks at you close, it's like nobody ever did.''

She made a sound that might have been a soft laugh or even a sigh and pressed her head against his shoulder. ''I never thought of it that way. And now that a big handsome hard-edge detective is paying attention to me, I should roll over and become his floozy.''

''I don't think I've ever heard anyone use that word.''

''We nuns tend to be antiquated, and sheltered, too.'' She rested a palm softly on his swollen penis. ''Whoa, what's this?''

''That's good luck.''

SHE said she didn't want to push her luck at Liberation House, though, so he dropped her off up the T-alley so nobody would see her sneaking back, and he drove straight up the Harbor Freeway to spend the night on Mike Lewis's sofa in the Arroyo. He didn't bother calling because Lewis never went to bed before two.

On his way through the four-level downtown he saw an 18-wheeler toppled on the third ramp up, the cab broken through the guard rail and dangling into space. Helicopters circled, playing searchlights on the truck. Something dark was dripping from level to level but hadn't hit the Pasadena yet. He was lucky to get through because the Highway Patrol was just setting up cones and flares.

The living room light shone out onto the drive.

''Jesus, Jack, where have you been? I did everything

but send up smoke signals. I thought you'd . . . Well, I was worried.''

''I didn't know you cared.''

''I'm glad you're still breathing, it's the way I like you best. Come look at something. You are now number one of the Find One Hundred Things Wrong With This Picture.''

Mike Lewis beckoned him over to the growing scatter of papers on the living room floor. ''Keep your voice down, Siobhan sleeps light. Your packet of goodies was laundered by someone, but they weren't careful enough.''

He stretched out his arms and lowered himself among the papers like Mephistopheles going down through the floor.

''Remember I said this little stage at the side of the blueprint was way too small for an opera house, and there weren't any flies for scenery and lighting. I was right. Here's another clue, down in the fine print of a memo.''

He looked where Lewis was pointing. The sentence said: . . . *as we discussed on the phone, we need something special to draw the punters in.*

''I know the word from England. It's a half contemptuous term for a small-time gambler. And then here.''

Jack Liffey followed the finger again. It was a letter from AT&T confirming the prices for conditioned landlines to two numbers, one in the 310 area code beginning with 419 and the other in 818 beginning with 514. ''That first one is Inglewood and the other is Arcadia. Ring any bells?''

''Inglewood's a relatively upscale black area and Arcadia is rich Republican dentists.''

''Think.''

"Maybe somebody's setting up orthodontia for all those shiny white teeth."

"A conditioned landline is a datalink. It's usually not for conversation but for digital information."

He certainly did have some annoying mannerisms, Jack Liffey thought. "I do know the words, Mike. We called them drops in aerospace, and we had them all over the building."

"I'll bet you didn't have them going to Santa Anita and Hollywood Park, though, did you?"

The phone rang and he leapt up nimbly.

Jack Liffey read the letter again, a chill forming along his legs and working its way up his spine. Lewis whispered into the phone, like a little emblem of the fear he felt all of a sudden. Dedicated lines to race tracks. He hadn't quite put it all together, but he had an idea of who he was probably up against now and he didn't like it.

Lewis came back and settled into a faded old sling chair from the 1950s. "You can probably guess what kind of place has small lounge stages, landlines to race tracks and talks about drawing the punters in. There's a few local option poker parlors in Gardena and Commerce and the Indian reservation out by Cabazon, but those are small potatoes. The state constitution tolerates what they call 'games of skill,' and the courts have always generously considered poker a game of skill. Must be knowing when to show 'em and when to fold 'em makes it a skill. Anyway, people have been trying to get full-bore gambling for years. Look at the size of that rubber factory. That would be the biggest casino west of Vegas, and within a forty-five-minute drive of ten million people."

The magic time in L.A.—everybody said a place was 45 minutes away, no matter how far it really was.

"I haven't heard anything about relaxing the laws for craps and roulette and slots, but who knows what agendas are grinding away in secret."

"Yeah," Jack Liffey said. "It could be important to some people to *stop* it, too. There's an awful lot of money invested in people driving more than forty-five minutes to do their gambling."

"Those are people you don't want to fuck with, is what I think," Lewis said simply.

"I already did."

Jack Liffey went straight to the phone. He noticed it was after one a.m. He called his own phone and listened to several messages, many of them from Mike Lewis. One was from Art Castro. "Oh, man, give me a call, please. I think you went and pissed on a nest of scorpions."

He called and got Castro's wife, sounding bleary.

"I'm sorry, Olga, this is Jack. You better wake him up."

It took a while, and when he came on he sounded slower than normal.

"I didn't mean call back at this hour, *hombre*."

"As long as you're up, how about filling me in?"

"Okay, sure, long as I'm up." He yawned with a little squeak at the end. "I got a friend in the body shop business. You know, they got a computer network these days, some of them, find parts from each other. Anyway, he saw where a M3 was getting some new windshield glass and he called over there for me. M3s not exactly falling out of the trees, probably of interest to you. These guys, they was getting all new tires, too, and as long as they was getting new rubber, they upgraded the tires, you know, went to the big ZRs for, like, driving one hundred and fifty and shit. Two hundred bucks a pop. They bought one for the spare, too, and the guy in the shop had to open the trunk and pull up the carpet to replace it. First thing he found in there, he found some Nevada plates wrapped in a rag. Had some dirt on them but pretty new. He'd been in Nam, this guy, and he knew what C-4 plastic explosive looks like. And everybody knows a Mac-11 with the long clip. These are bad dudes, *esse*."

"Okay, Art. Thanks. Leave it alone now. You never heard of me, and your friend in the chop shop never heard of you, too."

"It's not a chop shop, hey. I don't hang with no bangers. Good luck, man, really."

"Thanks." He hung up and saw Mike Lewis watching him. "You, too. Burn all that stuff and bury the ashes."

"You can't close Pandora's box, Jack."

"You damn well better hope I can."

"You got any protection?"

"You mean guns? A bit, but not here. What can you offer?"

Lewis considered. "You can borrow a 9mm Walther."

"Why not?"

He got it out of a shoe box in the hall closet, a shiny blued little automatic. "Here's the only thing you got to remember. This is the safety. You flick it up like this."

"*Jesus!*"

The exposed hammer fell as if the pistol was firing.

"Stupid hair-raising design. Germans engineers design everything for the convenience of the engineers. The first trigger pull after you use the safety is stiff because it has to recock. Okay?"

"Thanks. Let's hope I don't have to shoot anybody."

"It's a thought."

Lewis offered him a heap of bedding and he slept

fitfully on the sofa, with gusty rain lashing the uncurtained windows that looked out over the arroyo. Siobhan kissed him on the cheek on her way out in the morning, and Mike Lewis dragged himself out not long after.

"What's the weather out?" Jack Liffey asked.

"Look's like the rain's over for now. Does it matter?"

"Moisture matters. Here's why."

He borrowed a box of bandaids and Mike Lewis watched while he used them end-to-end to strap the pistol to his ankle so it held tight but would break away easily with a tug.

"Man, where did you learn that? That must be the state-of-the-art in detective craft."

"It was a Crimestopper. Very underrated, Mr. Tracy."

HE went straight to the Liberation House where a very worried young man met him at the front door.

"Can I speak to Eleanor?"

The boy blocked the door. "She never came home last night."

"Yes, she did. Why don't you go knock on her door."

"We've been in her room, man. We looked all over. Agnes'd've heard her on the steps. She never came in."

Jack Liffey's blood turned cold. "I dropped her off at midnight." He pushed past the boy, and the boy resisted for an instant and then fell away.

"I'm telling you, she isn't here."

Liffey strode up the stairs past a fretting older woman in a long kimono and went straight to Eleanor's room. The bed was more or less as he remembered them leaving it. He went to the small closet and racked the hangers back and forth. He had a clear picture of the striped blouse that he had folded so carefully and left on a damp white sage, and it wasn't there.

He went down the stairs and across the kitchen to the back door. The woman in the kimono padded after him without making a protest. Eleanor would have come in the back, just thirty yards from where he'd dropped her. Unless they'd been watching the back, waiting for her.

He kicked bundles of rags aside, but the doorlock fought him and he almost tore the door off its hinges. Then it swung open and he stopped in his tracks. There was a three-step concrete stoop leading down to a walk. Sitting in the middle of the stoop on the nubbly foot-wiper was a rubber rattlesnake.

14

OVERDETERMINATION

TIME TO GO HOME AND FACE THE MUSIC. IT WAS HIS FIRST lucid thought after seeing the rubber snake. Nothing cute like a gun on his ankle was going to be much help now. As he drove west, an overwhelming sense of despair hollowed him out. What on earth had he been thinking of? He had screamed a challenge into the dark doorway of a dream, and the nightmare had erupted out of the dark to swallow up someone he loved, as any sane man knew it would.

Up ahead, one of the Toonerville Trolleys was stopped on the elevated Green Line. People milled excitedly looking at something on the tracks. A man in a traindriver's uniform seemed to be kicking the side of the first car as hard as he could.

Then he was past the bridge and into the vast no-man's land of southeast L.A., where the poorest blacks and Central Americans lived side by side in gathering animosity. He tried to squeeze himself down, to become small and compact so that when the time came to act he would be ready.

He nodded absently to the guard going into the condo and parked in his usual spot beside the big Olds with the reflective AA stickers: *One Step at a Time* and *Take it Easy*. He took a roundabout route to an alcove where he could see his door. It wasn't kicked open. He considered flinging it open and hurling himself inside like some TV cop, but it was all too melodramatic so he just stepped in.

The light on his answering machine blinked rapidly, which meant it had malfunctioned again. Of course, it might not have been from Vegas. It might even have been from Kathy or Maeve, some minute readjustment of blame for his paternal failures.

He thought of walking to his office but decided to drive, in case he needed to move fast. He left the Concord facing out in the lot, just out of sight of Margolin's coffee counter.

The padlock was still on the crude hasp that held his boarded-up door, and beside it was a small yellow note. All it had was a phone number and a fat letter S. The initial might have stood for almost anything, but *snake* occurred to him right away, and when he looked closer, he saw that it was probably a crude drawing of a snake. He folded it into his pocket.

Downstairs Marlena was squatting beside a plastic tub of mail, sorting it into her boxes.

"Jack! I was worried." She stood and smoothed a tight skirt over her hips. "You didn't answer, all the time."

"I had to stay out of sight for a while."

She blocked his way so he had to hug her.

Very softly she said into his ear, "You're my only chance."

He shuddered. "There's a lot of people would jump in the L.A. River if I were their only chance."

"And some are more beautiful, I bet."

"That's not what I'm saying." He just couldn't attend to her now. "Can I make a call?"

"You know where it is."

She gave one long squeeze before turning him loose.

The number was a 310 and might have been almost anywhere on the periphery of the city.

"Yeah?"

"This is Jack Liffey. I got a note."

There was a moment of near silence, with only the electronic wheezes of phone devices talking to one another.

"Liffey, huh." It was a new voice, one that he recognized. "You got more wind on you than a little bull goin' uphill. My car insurance wants to talk to you. You want to help out your little filly, who's gone and got herself tied up, you'd best mosey this way. And, pard, don't even think about calling the sheriff."

They gave him an address that sounded like Cahuenga and hung up.

So, the worst was true after all. He stood with the phone in his hand, utterly incapable of moving. How had he signed up for this? An out-of-work technical writer, down on his luck and scrambling for cash in a mean city. Maybe he'd tried to even the odds a bit too hard, but this had turned out way beyond his sense of risk. He had to concentrate hard to move at all, not to run down into stasis. Hang up the phone, Jack.

"I've got to go somewhere," he told Marlena.

"Come back to me, *querido*." She hugged him from behind.

"Some real bad guys," he said. He looked up and saw a kid in a bright red T-shirt jumping up and down in the window, making faces. He couldn't work out whether the action had any meaning. "I think they're the ones who did the woman." He couldn't think of anybody's name he was so distracted. It took him a moment to remember the name Consuela, then Eleanor and finally Marlena. "I think I know why now."

"Can't you call the police?"

"It's my doing. I've got to undo it."

"Would money help you any?" she whispered, and the boy at the window redoubled his jumping, darting his tongue obscenely.

"Bless you for asking." He wrote down the address in Cahuenga and gave it to her. "I don't know if it will do any good but if I don't call you by eight tonight, go to a pay phone and send the fire department there. I don't think they'll be stupid enough to stay in the same place, but the fire guys are paid for driving around in their red trucks so you may as well use them."

As he started for the door, the boy fled.

"Don't you care that I'm afraid for you?" she asked querulously.

He looked back for a moment, trying to work out what she had said. "It means a lot." What means a lot? "Thanks, Marlena."

HE felt obliged to go straight to the address, though everything inside him begged to dawdle. It was ten and the roads were still clear, as if it took the drivers all morning and into the afternoon before they could work out how to get together to jam up the streets. He was more frightened than he'd ever been. The round had his name on it now, and he couldn't believe in things being off target. He remembered times, even in Nam, when death had seemed so far away that it was part of another life, but now it was close enough to touch.

He got stuck at a light behind a battered old round-fender pickup. The driver argued fitfully with someone who wasn't there. His head jerked and his right fist shot up and hit the cab roof, so hard Jack Liffey could hear the dull clang over the traffic noise. Then gems spewed away from his side window and the man's fist emerged into the sunlight for an instant. It took a moment before Jack Liffey realized what had happened. The man was having a bad morning of his own. With the light still red, the pickup lurched forward and fishtailed into a right turn, smoking a tire.

Jack Liffey looked down at the street, where glass fragments caught the sun. The incident had been sent by something or other to tear away the last fragments of normality. This was what the French philosophers called overdetermination. Reality poisoned you to death, stabbed you through the heart and then shot the corpse a few times. He wanted to be far away, somewhere safe and clean, where things behaved predictably, but what was coming seemed likely to be very close and inescapable and not very redeeming.

He started up again when a car honked at him. The sky eastward was scrubbed sparkling by the soft rains, and far in the distance he could see dark clouds over the mountains. A thunderhead climbed skyward, and a long line of planes marked the approach lane to LAX. He tried to fathom what had brought him to this exact spot, sinking along a trajectory he could not control. He had a tidiness streak in him, but this was too unruly to explain.

He could hear the rattle of his tappets. The engine needed oil, and the red light would come on in another hundred miles. It didn't seem to matter at all. In Cahuenga, he saw a couple of taxis like more ill omens. You never saw taxis in L.A. They were visible at the airport, but they evaporated from the universe as soon as they left it.

The address he'd been given was a small lot with a filthy mattress tented up in high weeds. Behind the mattress was a concrete foundation with a few charred two-by-fours where a house had been burned out. It looked vaguely familiar and then he saw the fading graffiti. *CINQUE RULES! Viva Tanya!* And, much smaller, *Down with imperialism and all its running dogs.* It must have been the cowboy's idea of a joke—this was the house where the Symbionese Liberation Army had holed up and cops from four jurisdictions had poured gunfire in until the building caught fire and burned. The fire department would get a big kick out of the joke if Marlena had to call them.

Up the street an extended family of Latinos were under the hood of an old Pontiac, some handing around parts and others pointing and tugging at things. Just then the BMW came around the corner and drove slowly up beside his car. The blacked passenger window whirred down and he saw the Cowboy only three feet away, looking at him neutrally The other man was driving.

The Cowboy's hand reached languidly out the window holding a large porcelain eagle. The bird was hand-painted in pastel colors, one of those horribly expensive statuettes from Germany that grandmothers bought from mail order ads. He held the eagle out at full stretch and rotated it once as if trying to sex it by peering in under the tail, then he let it go. It hit the pavement and broke cleanly at the base of a wing. Jack Liffey realized for the first time that something was wrong with the Cowboy's eyes. One of them was glass, but it was hard to tell which one.

"I got a new CD player built into the trunk," the Cowboy said mildly. "Carousel. Ten disks all stacked up and you play it through your stereo with a gizmo with a lot of buttons. Whenever I got somethin' broke up I always fix it up better than before or add on something. You see the point? You got to stay ahead of the curve.''

Jack Liffey saw his problem now—he'd only been trying to stay even, and everybody else was staying ahead.

The Cowboy got out and pressed the seat forward, jackknifing himself into the back of the M3. ''You get in front.''

It was all so civilized. Jack Liffey got in dully and they pulled away and drove for a minute before the Cowboy spoke again.

''When I was ten, the river up and flooded one wet spring. House was right on the bluff over the Brazos and the water come up to the front porch and me and pa spent all day out there killin' water moccasins that come up out of the river. We used .22s until we ran out of ammo and then baseball bats and a shovel. That's a true fact. Pa ran around crazy as a parrot eatin' stick candy, but I got so I liked the job. I got to teasin' 'em before I whacked 'em out. After a while I even got to think kindly on 'em a little. They was only doin' their nature. Still, I had to hit 'em. That was my nature.''

''The woman doesn't know a thing. You can let her go.''

''That so?''

''That's why I came quietly.''

''We ain't negotiatin' here. Just shut the fuck up now.''

There was dark cloud all around, but the car purred along in a charmed patch of brightness, light smarting the eye off the hood as if the gods had cleared a little space for their vengeful powers to work.

Crossing the river, he saw that the river had slacked off, only a foot or two of runoff moving down the central channel, then the car turned south and east into forsaken industrial land. They humped over railroad tracks into what a sign with a picture of an old glass milk bottle suggested had been a dairy and then they idled slowly along a dirt track cleared of rubble. Now and again the air dams hanging under the bumpers scraped on some upraised chunk of dirt. They stopped beside a low flat building that said *OFFICE*. Standing alone nearby was a plank shack that might have been yanked whole out of a deep mountain hollow in West Virginia.

"Get out," the Cowboy said.

Jack Liffey stepped out onto a little island of cement in a sea of mud. The Cowboy's friend locked up the car with a double-bleat of the car alarm and they walked to the office through sucking mud. There was a smell of manure in the air, and a faint deep noise, luring and anxious, maybe only a conception of noise as his mind tried to fill in the space, like the sound that a huge empty place makes in the distance. A gray curtain of rain had fallen over the mountains, and there was a tiny flashbulb flash in the thunderhead, too far to hear.

The Cowboy ducked inside and came back out, like someone going to the refrigerator for another beer.

"You're gonna have to hang around a bit, like a side a beef."

The other man had a big black pump shotgun now, and they took him to the shed where the Cowboy fought with a rusted padlock.

"You shouldn't never interfere with nothin' that don't bother you personal. You just smelt out the wrong hound's butt, pard."

It was dim inside and felt damp, smelling like chalky plaster. He went rigid when he saw Eleanor Ong lying on her stomach on a piece of stained carpet, her hands tied behind her back with an extravagant amount of rope. A tennis ball was duct-taped into her mouth. She rocked a little when she saw him, her eyes crazed, but he didn't see any evidence of wounds. She was still wearing the clothes he'd last seen her in.

When he looked up, the shotgun was on him.

"I'm not in this business to let diddlysquats shoot up my car. You get that yet?"

"I understand. You've got me now. How about letting her go?"

Without warning the Cowboy slapped him hard with his open palm so Liffey's head rocked back and his cheek caught fire.

"How about you keep the fuckin' shut up? You're only alive because my boss ain't made up his mind on you."

He took the shotgun, and the other man tied Jack Liffey's hands behind him. They dragged him across the room and tied a loose end of the rope to the trap pipe under a basin. He was on his knees on the concrete floor with the basin tight in his back.

The Cowboy turned the shotgun around and rested the butt against Jack Liffey's cheek. The rubber butt-plate felt warm.

"Just be happy I don't give you a little quick dentistry, tough guy." He laughed dismissively. They left, and Jack Liffey could hear the padlock snapping down.

He looked at Eleanor. "I'm sorry I got you in this," he said mournfully. "I didn't know it would go so bad."

A chink of blue showed through the roof and it was all he could do to keep from looking at it. Like the bright eye at the far top of a deep well. One more horror was all he needed.

"Can you nod or shake your head?" Her head barely moved. She made a series of tortured noises and he guessed the duct tape was caught in her hair and made it painful to move. "Did they hurt you? Make one noise for yes, or two for no."

She made a kind of groan from deep in her throat. She clearly made it twice.

"Did they grab you last night when I dropped you off?"

Yes.

"You came straight here?"

Yes. Tears were now running down her cheeks.

"Did they ask you anything?"

No.

"Did they try to get you to do anything?"

No.

"They just tied you up and left you?"

Yes.

"Has anyone looked in this shack at all since then?"

He established that the Cowboy's friend had fed her in the morning and led her once to a bathroom in the office. They'd taped the ball in her mouth after she'd started screaming out the bathroom window. Eventually the twenty questions ran out.

"I messed it up," he said lamely. "I'm sorry."

She made a whole string of noises, but he couldn't work out what she was trying to say. "I don't think they'll do anything terrible. They'd have done it already." He wasn't as confident as he tried to sound, and he didn't know whether she believed him. They both knew what had happened to Consuela Beltran.

His wrists hurt and he was losing sensation in his knees. His eye caught again on the chink of light overhead and his whole body went tense, sweat breaking out on his forehead. How could an irrational memory-fear even register against so much real fear?

He forced his attention away from the oblong of sky. One of the rafter beams seemed serrated and he stared hard at the row of lumps until he worked out that they were the carcasses of rats, nailed up one after another. Was it voodoo? Why would you crucify rats? They were of all sizes and looked mummified. He wondered if his sense of reality was being subverted.

"I love you," he said to her.

She made a steady choked sobbing, like a seizure, her head bobbing in tiny spasms.

The padlock rattled.

Let me do the talking, he thought, nearly delirious with fear. He saw now how people went mad; they just refused to look straight at things any more. Powerlessness was the worst thing there was.

Light flooded in and the Cowboy's shape waited a moment against the light. As Jack Liffey's eyes adjusted he could see that the sky was all dark cloud. A doom sky.

"Well, stud-duck, the boss checked in about you and he was mad enough to kick a hog barefoot."

"I've destroyed all the papers," Jack Liffey said. "There's no reason for anyone to be after me."

"I'm sure you're right, pardner. I really am. I'm sure you'd love to wear out a few more saddles before checking out of the corral, but, the thing is, how are we going to trust you? You see? It's really pretty tough to see how we could wish you well."

The other one came in and tugged Eleanor to her feet.

"I wonder if you're good at the big mysteries," the Cowboy said. "Every swinging dick wants to know the answers and now you get to. That's the nut, really."

15

THE WHOLE WEIGHT OF THE CITY

THE TWO HOODS MARCHED THEM ACROSS THE WASTE ground. He tried to figure out where they were being herded so he could come up with a plan, anything at all to give him some hope, but the only thing he saw ahead was a ragtag corrugated metal shed against the far fence and he didn't really think they'd get that far. He tried to make himself some luck but he couldn't work the trick. Now and again puddles sucked at his feet, and he tried not to look at Eleanor Ong. Seeing her only made him feel more unlucky.

"We gotta be at Johnny's at one," the man with the shotgun said.

"*Shutup.* Well, pard, I made you out tougher than a long-tail catamount and you and me mighta got on, some other life." He laughed. "You don't wanna hear that. I guess I was just raised up on prunes and proverbs."

"What are you after, absolution?" Jack Liffey snapped.

"We just do our job and then we leak out of this here landscape."

All of a sudden, the shotgun came up to bar their way. The Cowboy yanked the duct tape off Eleanor, a good hank of hair coming away with it, and she cried out and then gulped air as the tennis ball bounced incongruously away into the mud. Jack Liffey was jerked backwards, and the two hoods lashed them together back to back. He could feel her shuddering as she sobbed.

The Cowboy's friend handed off the shotgun and bent over at a rusty steel trapdoor set in concrete at their feet. The door squealed as it swung up, and a chill swept out from whatever was below.

"There we at," the Cowboy's friend said.

"Sorry, you two. Pa always said the best bet for crossing the river was to sink to the bottom and run like hell."

Jack Liffey could hear the whisper of running water down there somewhere and he smelled fermenting leaves.

It was the playground trick again. One of them kicked the back of his knees so his legs buckled as the other shoved Eleanor. The earth was no longer underfoot and they plummeted into the dark like rocks. She screamed, but his voice had frozen up, he was trying so hard to keep his legs beneath him. His shoulder scraped concrete. He howled when his elbow glanced hard off something. He was sure it had cut him badly and then they hit water, followed almost instantly by the hard beneath the water.

The pain in his arm was intense and there was a new pain in both ankles. When the splashing panic was over he found himself upright in cold water that was only up to his thighs. Eleanor was a dead weight trying to tug him over backwards. Far above there was a blob of light, and after a single glance at it, he couldn't think straight.

"Nine-point-nine, degree of difficulty," he heard faintly and then the voice boomed into echo. The steel trap gnashed shut and the light snuffed out.

Darkness was actually an improvement. He pressed his good shoulder against the wall to keep himself located in the dark, then leaned forward to make sure Eleanor's slumping head stayed out of the water. Briefly he had seen the layout of their surroundings, a concrete box cut through by a horizontal storm drain maybe three feet in diameter. The water came about half way up the drain. There'd only been drizzle nearby, but he had seen the thunderheads on the mountains and he had no idea how many drains led into this one. He knew now how Consuela Beltran had ended up washed down into the pool at the Queen Mary. He wondered how long her body had drifted through the drains and how many branches it had followed.

"Eleanor. Eleanor!"

He thought he heard a sob.

"*Eleanor.*"

"It hurts so bad."

She jerked against him and he was elated that she was alive. She made a tiny screech when he moved, and he could almost see the sound of her voice flying up the concrete silo to rap once against the steel door at the top. He dragged her weight against the wall and the movement made a thousand echoes of splashing.

"*Oh, Lorsy.* I think my leg's broke."

"I've got a Swiss army knife in my front right pocket." Don't ask, he thought, tell. Leave no options. If either of them started thinking, they would panic and then they would begin to die. "I want you to take it out and hold it, and I'll open a blade."

She fumbled toward his left pocket.

"The *other* right."

She sniffled as he torqued himself around, and her hands felt over him. "Is that a pickle in your pocket or are you just happy to see me?"

It took him a moment to realize what she'd said. He owed her a laugh, he thought, a really big one some time, but not now.

"I got it. I feel a lumpy thing on it."

"That's the corkscrew. It's on the backside. Hold the other side to my hands." There was a short blade, a long blade, a combination screwdriver and bottle cap lifter, a can opener, and a pathetic little scissors. He thought he could find the long blade by feel. And then he heard the splash and her little sob.

"*I dropped it*. I'm sorry, I'm sorry." Hysteria skirled through her voice.

"It's okay. Just squat against me and we'll slide down the wall. It'll take the weight off your leg anyway."

They inched their shoulders down the concrete until their legs gave out all at once, splatting them down heavily. The chest-high water had a rich smell up close, like mown grass and old iced tea.

"Bounce a bit in my direction." He patted the slime under him with his bound hands as they heaved their buttocks along. He sucked a breath, pretty sure he'd cut himself on a piece of broken glass, and then he found the knife almost five feet downstream. The fall and all the wrenching around had loosened his hands enough so he could pry out the blade by himself. It was only a moment to saw the two of them apart.

He felt her bonds carefully, the lay of the rope against her wrists and then he found a spot to insert the blade and cut upward.

"Oh, I got it I got it I got it I got it."

"Take the knife and cut my hands loose. Careful. It's very sharp."

The first thing they did when their hands were free was hug. "I prayed," she said. "I prayed for you. I can't believe we're still alive. I'm not any good at this at all.''

"You're doing fine."

"All I wanted out of life was a little more life and I got this. Jack, at one point I was so scared I wanted them to go on and kill me to get it over. It must be a terrible sin to pray to die."

He had to think and he had to calibrate his fear carefully so it drove him on without taking him over. "We can't go back up here," he said. "Even if that cover's not locked, they'd see us and throw us down again."

"Are you going to save us now?" she said with an odd twist. "Is that what the tough detective is good for?"

He didn't want to deal with that. "We've got to go downstream to the next manhole. It can't be far."

He felt her stiffen. "I can't crawl into a pipe."

"It's not that far."

A three-foot conduit, on hands and knees, maybe two hundred yards. Crawling in the darkness with the whole weight of the city crushing down on them and a flood coming any time.

"Maybe ten minutes. A lot of Jews in Warsaw crawled through a smaller pipe for hours on end to escape the ghetto after the uprising failed."

He could feel his tension holding at the edge of panic, like the sensation of drowning. *Okay, we're climbing straight up the shaft!* he thought, but he fought back the urge. Blank out your mind and crawl, he told himself. He slid his hand down the wall, hunting out the upper lip of the conduit. A shudder took him when he realized how small it was. Kneeling, their backs would almost graze the top of the pipe. The water had receded a bit, as if a drain plug had been pulled, and it rippled past shin-deep, a little more than a foot. He brought his head down and heard the hollowness. He was surprised by a faint glow, a hint of definition to the curve of the pipe far away.

She sobbed with fear and he reached back over his shoulder to touch her.

"Hush. There's some light."

"This is *awful*. It's too small."

"We can do it."

"What if there's water?"

"We'd be pushed ahead of it," he said, "and we could go up the next manhole." Or they could body surf all the way to the L.A. River, he thought. The problem would be breathing. His mind entertained a terrible image of being carried along by a surge and then slammed against a steel grill high above the river, pinned there in some awkward posture by the tons of water gushing past.

They say drowning is quite pleasant; you just take a deep breath of water and slip into oblivion.

Who say?

Well, obviously not people who drowned.

She hugged his back hard and gave a series of rising squeals in the dark, thrusting her hips against him, and he thought she might be lost to panic.

"Oh, dear. I'm sorry."

"What do you mean?"

"I had an orgasm. I didn't mean to."

"It's okay, but save me a few for later. Let's go."

She wriggled out of his way, and he knelt into the cold water which rustled and whispered eerily in the pipe.

"*Jack!*"

"Here we go."

He shuffled into the storm drain, knee and hand, knee and hand. The pipe was made of a smooth ceramic with joins every ten feet or so. He could feel twigs and light bobbing chunks, probably plastic cups, and there was a smelly foam carried along by the current.

"It's not so bad," he called. "Don't dawdle." The water ran fast. Something sharp hit his leg from behind and he spread his legs to let it pass. The pipe's surface was smooth and cool just above the water line but gritty under the water, and his palm tended to lose purchase on the shallow curve.

"I can't do it."

"Let's go, dammit."

He heard her set out at last, intoning something rapidly, some Catholic formula for self-hypnosis. He crawled mechanically, tiring himself with the tension of it all, trying to blank his mind against waves of claustrophobic horror.

Her rosary soon gave out. "That prayer used to bring me peace."

He felt a spray and heard a different hollowness in one ear. Reaching up, he discovered an opening where a small pipe emptied into the storm drain at head level, pouring water over a crust of lime.

"Even after I stopped believing." Her monologue competed with the high-pitched rustlings of the water. He couldn't really follow her but he sensed she was just talking to keep from thinking.

"I got used to knowing there wasn't anything. That was okay for a long time. . . ."

Left hand and right knee, right hand and left knee. Horses did it, but was it called a canter? A gallop? The water rush changed pitch, and his full attention turned to the new sounds.

"Then this damn hope came back."

The pace was punishing, like trying to stay afloat in a pool on pure energy. Again and again he dragged his mind back from images of the pipe collapsing or filling with water.

"Hope destroyed my peace."

The water became less whispery and felt faster.

"Hush," he said.

"Now I wonder if I was just sick all that time I was comforted."

He wanted to listen to the water's chat and murmur.

"Maybe the peace was a kind of sickness. It was peace that was unnatural."

Less of his thigh was lifting out of the water as he slid forward. Was it his imagination? Far ahead he could see the source of the light, a faint color change at the top of the conduit that probably marked the oval of a vertical shaft. Escape.

"It's up to my elbows," she announced in horror.

It wasn't, but it was definitely rising. Another pipe joined from the side, a fine cold stream splashing over his cheek, then wetting his shoulder, finally his hips. In a moment he heard her gasp and spit water.

Then the water did reach their elbows. He tried to convince himself the rise was only from the feeder pipes they passed, and those puny streams wouldn't raise the level much more.

"*Jack!*"

He heard the faint roar behind them, an animal loosed into the storm drain. There could be no going back against the current, but he resolved to make the manhole before it arrived.

"We're almost there," he lied.

The roar drew closer, chasing away all other sounds. His mind was busy fighting the panic: *go on, scream and give it up*.

The light was so faint he was afraid of overrunning

the manhole so every few strides he slapped at the top of the pipe.

"Oh my God, oh my God," she wailed.

The water dragged at his arms and thighs as he tried to hurry, and then the water level teased his belly. He visualized a narrow band of air trapped in the top of the pipe. Would it stay? He was assailed by a mental picture of the manhole he had seen as a boy, down near the ocean, the cover blown off late in a storm and water spouting into the air.

Eleanor cried out as if struck.

Water buoyed him and he was half dog-paddling, half hurled along, his head scraping the top. Panic breathed into his ear. She might have screamed but the sound was lost in the boom of a train through a tunnel.

"Here it is!" he cried out. He fought for something to grab in the shaft overhead. There was blessed light. His fingers scrabbled against concrete and the water pressure was pitiless. The flow dragged his legs past, flipping him onto his back so that his fingers strained to hold onto the last edge of the shaft. He heard her hacking wet cough. Then a ton of elbows blasted into him and tore him loose so the two of them swept into darkness, gathering momentum.

"Cling to me! Keep your face forward!"

He was disoriented as he surfed along, feet first, and the oily foam made it hard to breathe. Sticks and debris floated alongside his face and something clung to his shoulder, buffeting, trying to drag him down. It took a tremendous act of will to keep from hammering his fists into her. Her nails bit into his neck, and the rage became primitive as he lost orientation: she was taking away his one chance.

He breathed through the fingers of one hand, trying to keep out the slime. There were only a few inches of air in the top curve of the pipe now. He saw a flash of light and heard a momentary booming—an echo from a direction he only realized was up when they were past. They'd swept past the next manhole. The nightmare image came again: pinned flat to a grille of steel bars as water boiled past them. The incredible *pressure* of all that water behind.

Her grip on him weakened. He cried out as they hit the wall at a curving reach in the storm drain. There was a flash, either real light, or some artifact of the blow, and then he found a metal rung in his hand, startling with its solidity. He pawed desperately with the other hand.

He got both hands on the crusty metal, and still the water tried to tear him loose, pulling on his legs with an impossible force. It must have been Eleanor's deadweight clinging somehow to his leg. His palms burned. He tore his head out of the foam into an airspace, gasped one clear breath and shouted with relief. He wanted to kick his legs free of her, kick off the killing tug. The impulse was almost irresistible.

Control! By pulling with all his strength and thrusting with his free leg, he wrenched himself around until he was sitting upright in a small manhole shaft, head and shoulders out of the water as the current streamed hard past his hips. He made the immense mental effort to force himself to release the rung with one hand and reach down to the deadweight. He pawed for anything to grab. His hand slid off what must have been a bare shoulder, rejected her hair, and finally closed on a thick brassiere strap. He found a reserve of strength somewhere and for one terrible instant used both hands to drag her forward. Finally her head broke the surface. He wedged her body between himself and the edge of the shaft and let the water and debris thunder past.

He gasped for a moment, allowing himself a moment of peace. Far overhead there were three pinholes of light. As the panic subsided, his eyes adjusted to what might have been Eleanor Ong's immobile face. She didn't seem to be breathing. He barked out a snarl of frustration, a sound he had never made before and hardly recognized as his own. In despair he began to press her chest against the tunnel edge and release it, no more than a token of artificial respiration. Set her adrift, a tiny voice said. Climb out. You did what you could. You're absolved. He thought he saw a ghostly shoulder covered with lacerations, bleeding darkly into the current, but he wasn't sure.

He swore. He cursed. In anger he shook her shoulder. She felt clammy and cold.

"Eleanor!"

He slapped her face hard and abruptly a spasm took her body. She rolled her head around and vomited. Then she shuddered and coughed, pawing him with sudden strength. He placed her hands on the rung between his.

"Hang on, hang on."

He babbled and laughed wildly, had no idea what he was saying. It was a miracle! She was alive! They'd have to say rosaries for years to make up for this! She went on retching for a long time, until she ebbed back into a steady sobbing.

It was time to get out. He helped her get her arms up two rungs and then boosted her two more, but she would never make it any farther under her own power. He could see a white flash of bone and realized she had a compound fracture half way up her lower leg. She must have been in shock for a long time. He got his head between her thighs to lift her piggy-back another rung. Then another. She was heavy.

"I love you, God," she said deliriously. Who was it

she loved? Him or God? "I've never loved like this."

Straining with legs and arms he hoisted her rung by rung, and she pulled her upper body along as best she could. The boom of the water diminished.

"We'll make it, we will."

Finally she uttered an excited grunting, like a mute. Her head had reached the manhole and the three bright eyes showed through. He could tell she would never have the strength to lift the manhole cover by herself and he used his hands to plant her good foot firmly on a rung. Then he fought around her in the confining shaft, noticing for the first time that her blouse had disappeared somewhere and her shoulder really was lacerated. He heaved against the cover, but nothing moved.

He caught his breath, panting like a wrestler, and planted himself firmly. He couldn't fail now. He put all his strength into a thrust, and finally heard a metallic complaint. The manhole lid broke free and clanged an inch to one side. One more shove and light flooded in, the sky overcast and raining but the cool air delicious of amnesty.

Were they far enough from the dairy? He slid the cover again, not really caring where they were as long as they were out of the storm drain. He boosted up onto his belly and then he was outside, lying on a deserted wet street. He reached back for her hand and forearm. Her head rose out of the manhole, gasping in the wonderful cool air. He hauled her out.

"Holy Mary, Mother of God, pray for us sinners now and in the hour of our . . ."

For almost a minute he lay laughing softly as she said her prayers and then they both ran down.

"I was tough enough," he said with relish. "And I owe you a laugh for your joke."

"Huh?"

''The pickle in my pocket.''

She just shook her head slowly, and he realized she was delirious and didn't remember much of anything. She was bedraggled and bleeding and pale, and he saw her watching him with a curious tenderness. She set one palm against his cheek. She smiled gently, and later he would blame himself for not demanding an explanation for what she said.

''I don't think you're going to make it,'' she said.

16

TIME TO ROCK AND ROLL

HE SAT WITH HIS RIGHT LEG CRANKED ACROSS HIS LEFT knee, rewrapping the Ace bandage. The whole right ankle was black as ebony under the skin where the ligaments had torn. The left wasn't a picnic, either, and it had its own Ace. By noon the joints usually got used to the new dispensation and stopped complaining as much. Codeine helped, too.

He was a lot better off than Eleanor Ong who was at Hollywood Presbyterian-Queen of Angels, trussed up in traction like a spitted roast. They weren't letting her see anyone yet. He wondered idly what happened when they merged a Presbyterian hospital with a Catholic hospital, if the nuns had to work in pairs with dour Scots nurses so they'd nullify each other.

"Ow!"

What the ankle didn't like was a lateral twist.

The future was still in the balance. He was beset by a kind of manic-depression that yawed from moment to moment. One moment it was enough to be alive, and the next everything felt precarious again. There were two men somewhere in the city who thought he and Eleanor were dead and would be more than happy to rectify their error once they found out about it. If he dropped a dime on them, there'd just be two different guys a week later.

The violent physical ordeal had left its calling card of mortality. He found he was locked into a profound unease that made him want to go hide in a closet. He took four ibuprofens, an anti-inflammatory dose, and lumbered around his living room with his face screwed up. Mild pain was salutary if you calibrated it carefully. Discomfort was the no-man's-land where ideas germinated.

The doorbell startled him. It was a clumsy mechanical device that you worked by twisting a big thumbscrew on the outside, but he rarely heard it because the guard was supposed to call ahead.

He saw immediately that it was a cop of some stripe. The man wore a dark suit and skinny black tie and he let a leather ID wallet dangle open that said he was FBI. The eyes under the crew cut were as dead as rocks.

"I'm Special Agent Curtis Cobb. Are you Jack Liffey?"

"I thought you guys traveled in pairs."

"May I come in?"

He thought about refusing, but there was no percentage in it. "You guys all *special* agents? Any of you ordinary agents?"

Cobb stepped in, looking around with a glance that didn't seem to see much but was probably going faster than an adding machine.

"I've got coffee going."

He expected a refusal, but the agent nodded. "I wouldn't say no. Is it strong?"

"You can stand the spoon up in it."

He went to pour two cups.

"You've got a limp, Mr. Liffey."

It wasn't a question, so he didn't answer.

"Milk? Sugar? Sweet 'N Low?"

"Black. Were you injured? It looks like *both* ankles. That's unusual."

Let's see who blinks first, Jack Liffey thought. "What's on your mind? Go on, sit down."

The FBI man sat on a director's chair and Jack Liffey handed him the coffee and then swung a hard chair around so he'd be about two inches higher.

"The police in Cahuenga say you were looking into the murder of Consuela Beltran."

He waited. It was shaping up as an extended duel of politenesses, and the FBI man was beginning to glare a little.

"This touches on an ongoing investigation of ours. You really have no shield protection to keep from telling us what you know. You don't want to screw around with us, Mr. Liffey, you really don't."

He thought about that for a moment. He was right, he really didn't want to screw around with them. He just wanted a level playing field.

"I find missing kids, it's what I do. I found Mrs. Beltran's boy once, a couple years ago, and brought him home. Then Mrs. Beltran went missing and her mom came up from Mexico and asked me to find her, but when it turned into murder, I figured to butt out."

"But you didn't butt out right away, did you?"

"Murder is for the cops."

Cobb went to the inner pocket of his coat. It turned out to be two small photographs which he leaned to hand across—the Cowboy and his friend, mug shots with numbers under their chests. It was nice to see them that way.

"The first is Bobby O'Connor, lately of Navasota, Texas. They call him Snakeskin." That was the Cowboy. "The other one is Al Butera, they call him Squinty.

He's not much, but he's company for Snakeskin."

"Colorful names," Jack Liffey said.

"They work for one of the families in New York. These two aren't made men or anything. Even Butera. He's Sicilian, somebody or other's cousin, but the only way he'd get into the Mafia is if they went to affirmative action. They're just mechanics. You know what that means?"

He nodded. It was what he figured. There would always be a couple more hired thugs on deck.

"I think you had a run-in with these two. They messed up your office. Then you hit their car. Sort of a Laurel and Hardy routine." He seemed to like the coffee, but he had nowhere to put down the cup. Jack Liffey had seen to that. "You ever see the two-reeler about the Christmas tree salesmen? It's that guy with the mustache and he slams the door on their tree. Then they fume a bit and Laurel scratches his head and Ollie tears off the guy's porch light. The guy with the mustache does a slow burn and then marches out and dents their car. Pretty soon he's wrenching fenders off and they're throwing his piano out the window."

"I can see you don't have a lot to do all day in the Bureau."

"Looking at your ankles, I figure there's a few tits-for-tats we don't know about."

Jack Liffey remembered the two thugs talking about having to get permission. "Who's their boss?" he asked.

Cobb perked up a little at the direct question. It gave him an opportunity to come back and swing his dick a little. "We're not in the business of disseminating information. You want to help us?"

"I already did."

"I can tell you that the case you butted into relates to the big-time casinos, not the kind that hire overweight washed-up singers for their lounge acts. There's a lot of people want to see that action stay in Vegas and there's others want to spread it around. The last casino built in Vegas cost over a billion dollars. You don't want to stand between these guys.''

"I think we pretty much agree on that. How do I convince them I'm out?''

"That's a good question. I think the first mistake you made was getting involved with no way of covering your butt. The second mistake was making the first mistake. Do you know something that can hurt them?''

Jack Liffey just stared back, watching the FBI man trying not to fidget with the coffee cup.

"It doesn't really matter. What matters is whether they *think* you can hurt them. If they do, you've got a real problem. Maybe not the kind of problem you'd have if they was Colombians. Those guys would level Culver City to get you, they'd strap an A-bomb to your newsboy. These guys are rational, but they don't give up.''

"What are you offering me? Witness protection?''

"I think it could be arranged, if you know something that could put these two and a couple more like them behind bars.''

"Live in Dubuque. Call myself Joe Schmo.'' After all, he thought, what did he have left to hold him? Kathy wouldn't even let him talk to Maeve on the phone. He certainly didn't have much of a job. He had a tiny condo with a ridiculous forty-year mortgage that, after the L.A. real estate collapse, was worth a lot less than he owed on it. He had a fifteen-year-old car that wouldn't get him as far as the suburbs. Eleanor might even be willing to move with him.

Still, his identity inhabited a certain space in the world. How could he let someone chase him out of it?

He'd spend the rest of his life in a made-up space. He grimaced. It was not one of his options.

"I like my name. Sorry."

The FBI man finally set the cup down on the floor. He spread his arms wide as if appealing to a whole congregation of Jack Liffey's personalities.

"What's a name? Pick another river. Ireland's got plenty of them. Has this city been so great to you, you want to die prematurely here?"

"It's got its moments."

He'd lived with generalized anxiety for a long time, riding it up and down hill with his moods, he'd even got about as used to it as you ever could. This might not be much worse if he worked it right.

"You're gonna be in some heavy-duty shit, you know. Even if we bust Snakeskin and Squinty for something else. Their boss is gonna want a clear field."

"You couldn't tell me his name? Just an initial? I could guess and you could whinny when I get close."

"Names wouldn't do you any good." He stood up. "I can tell when a guy's got his mind made up. I'll stop back by if their aim is off the first time, make sure you're still plugged into the breathing machine at County. Might change your mind. Who knows, you might get lucky."

"I'm counting on it."

THERE was a big sign on the reception wall, the kind with the background etched away to leave raised letters: "Assets Located. Bodyguards. Child Custody. Debugging. Embezzlement. Executive Protection." It went on and on for four columns, through "Inventory Shortages" and "Mergers, Acquisitions" and "Questionable Documents" to "And Most Other Matters."

"Can I help you?"

"I'm here about Most Other Matters," Jack Liffey said to the woman, whose blue eyes were already narrowing. He seemed to be passing through a manic phase. She wore a conservative green dress and her hair was punished back into a tight hairdo that looked as if it had been yanked down by a rototiller. This had to be Ellen.

"Art Castro is expecting me."

"You'd be Jack Liffey," she said.

A tiny scrupulous voice echoed inside him that he should really only challenge the powerful, but gatekeepers had always annoyed him out of proportion. Their usurpations and assumptions.

"I would be, if everything worked." He looked down at his ankles. "I'm running about half a Liffey."

"Please have a seat."

He sat and thumbed through a month-old *Sports Illustrated*. There was nothing else. A nineteen-year-old seven-footer brought in from Italy was having trouble getting used to Salt Lake City. Some petite swimmer was making sure her nipples showed through the spandex. A washed-up quarterback was opening a cattle ranch in Wyoming. It was like reading random messages from another universe.

"Jack, come on back."

Art Castro leaned into the waiting area, the tidy mustache looking painted on his round face. Jack Liffey followed him down the corridor.

"Did she announce me?"

"No. It's one of her penalties. She would have, sooner or later."

"Remind me to stay on her good side."

Art Castro laughed softly. "She keeps out the riffraff."

"So you only work for people who don't need you. It's a concept."

In the office, a tiny chihuahua was vibrating and panting in the center of the rug.

"Good grief."

Art Castro frowned. "Calm down, Pedro. My aunt
asked me to pick him up from the vet's."

At least it wasn't named for a Cuban revolutionary.
Jack Liffey sat in a hard chair near the desk, and the
dog took an immediate liking to his scuffed shoe, licking
and sniffling at it.

"They're wound too tight," Art Castro said.

"I wonder what they were bred for? What could they
possibly do?"

"The variety within the dog species is unique among
mammals," Art Castro said pedantically. Now and then
he liked to remind you he had a college degree. "What
this one is good for you'll have to ask a mesolithic man
from the Sonoran Desert. Or my mesolithic Aunt Ce-
cilia."

Jack Liffey kept thinking of the scene from Tolstoy
where the overbearing countess snatched the cigar from
the general's mouth and tossed it out the window of the
moving train, and without missing a beat the general
snatched her lapdog and sent it after the cigar.

The dog crooned and began fucking Jack Liffey's
foot.

"Hold on, there, pal."

Art Castro sighed and scooped it up, then set it down
on top of a filing cabinet. The dog went rigid with its
forelegs stiff, gnarring rhythmically like a cicada.

They talked politely for a while about the smog,
about the decline in property values, and the tendency
of people to hide away in their own gated neighbor-
hoods.

"There won't be any public land left. We already
haven't got any parks. This city is shameful on parks."

"We've got beaches."

"*You* got beaches. Browns and blacks are marooned inland."

"Maybe the Big One will come along and move the shoreline inland a few miles."

The dog mewled and started snapping its tiny jaws.

"What can I do for you?" Art Castro said finally.

"I want to send you a package to hold. It's the usual kamikaze sort of rules. I don't want you to open it unless something tragic happens to me, then you'll find instructions on what to do inside."

Art Castro cocked his head, without replying. He looked around at the dog, which had gone quiet again, then back at his hands which he opened in front of him as if inspecting whether they were holding anything.

"You sound like you're in trouble."

"I can't tell you the what-fors, Art. I need this. I'm sorry."

"I've never known this sort of thing to do much good, but you call the shots."

"How do I keep your secretary from opening it when the postman drops it off?"

He rubbed one eye. "Well, if you write *Private and Confidential* on it, you can pretty well bet she'll open it." He dug in his desk and finally came up with a card. "Send it here."

The card simply said AC Enterprises and had a P.O. box in Bell Gardens. "It's a front I keep."

Jack Liffey memorized the number and the zip and handed the card back. "Thanks."

"You're giving me the bads. Can't I help?"

"I don't think you want to get involved. I'm hoping this is a way out, not a way in deeper. Okay?"

"Don't worry about sounding innocent on my account. I know you're not one of the bad guys."

There was a tiny sound of water and Art Castro glanced around. Dog pee dripped over the edge of the filing cabinet and the smell was remarkably strong all of a sudden, like opening an old box you found in the back garden.

"Shit."

"I've got to go."

"Abandon me in my hour of trial." He shook Jack Liffey's hand. "You're a great kidder, Jack. I hope this works out."

IT was a seedy-looking bar, driven to outlandishness by the sideshow crowd who'd spilled in from a carny site nearby. A midget with a big head was perched precariously on a bar stool, talking to a man who was over six feet tall and couldn't have broken a hundred pounds. He looked as if he'd been assembled out of a dozen No. 2 pencils.

The midget waved flamboyantly. "So the Devil goes, 'You got to give up your soul at the end,' and the lawyer goes, 'Sure, no problem, man, but I don't get it, what's the catch?'"

The skinny man threw his head back and laughed in a rapid staccato that reminded Jack Liffey of the chihuahua.

"Could I get a beer? Whatever's on tap."

Ten minutes earlier, nobody had been at the old dairy, just tire marks in the mud, but it didn't have the look of a place that had been cleared out. On the way there he'd seen the carnival tents going up, and the activity drew him back, like good dense cover for a duck shoot. Berkov's Fun-o-Rama, the trailers and trucks had said in garish reds and golds. He was careful not to let any of the guns show.

"How did the great DiMaggio do today?" somebody cried out in a terrible Cuban accent.

"Honey, I'm home. And you gotta lot a' 'splainin' to do."

An overweight bartender waggled his eyebrows a few times as he set a waspwaist beer glass in front of Jack Liffey. "You wanna run a tab?"

"Sure. You know anything about the old dairy down on Gleason?"

"We don't serve a lot of milk."

"Water either, I bet," the pencil man butted in. "You know why W. C. Fields never drank water?"

The midget giggled. "No, why did W. C. Fields never drank water?"

"Because, sez Mr. Fields, fish fuck in it."

They both thought that was uproarious. Jack Liffey had heard it, but smiled politely. "I just wonder how long the dairy's been vacant."

"Long as I can remember," the bartender said. "You got a reason to ask?"

"I know somebody looking for land around here. Know who owns it now?"

"Who knows? Probably the Arabs."

"I see somebody in a BMW coming and going. Must be planning to do something with the land."

"Are you a cop?" A little wave of stillness spread outward from the bar, heads cocked for the reply.

"Nah, I'm an insurance agent. You know, it's amazing how many people don't know the advantages of term insurance. I'll bet you're seriously underinsured on your accident and personal liability. You take your average person, now, they haven't even got a private supplement for disability." That was dull enough to turn the buzz loose again. Even the pencil man sitting next to him lost interest.

The bartender remembered something that needed his attention down the bar. There was nothing any of them knew that would help him. He knew what he had to do, and he only needed to prepare himself. They said scared money never wins, but he was betting on it. You couldn't rely on courage. Sooner or later everyone failed in courage. All you could rely on was worrying things to death.

"Buy us a drink?" the pencil man said.

"What's yours?"

"Cognac."

It was beer glasses in front of the midget and the pencil man, but Jack Liffey shrugged. "Two cognacs," he called along the bar. It was bad karma to make new enemies now. There were a dozen other people drinking in the room, a pair of bearded twins with heads a size too small, a big woman with breasts bobbling under a lacy shirt, and a lot of fairly normal-looking men with tattoos.

"You *is* a cop, ain't you?" the pencil man insisted. "Insurance is just blowin' smoke up our ass."

"Nope."

"I can smell 'em."

"How come you're not helping set up the tents?"

"We're talent. Talent don't get paid to sweat. You know why I don't like cops?"

"You don't need a reason. Nobody likes cops."

He drew himself up to a kind of dignity. "Cops're all trained to see evil and so that's all they see. It's like doctors, they just see disease everywhere. I happen to believe people are inherently good inside."

The midget guffawed. "Nietzsche was wrong. It's the devil who's dead."

The bartender brought snifters of cognac and the pencil man nodded his thanks. The midget bent forward, kneeling on the stool, to inhale the aroma over the snifter, and he broke into a wide grin as if reminded of something rapturous in his youth.

"Can I get a marshmallow? I always drink cognac with a marshmallow." No one paid him any attention.

"You know, I ain't bulimic," the pencil man insisted. "You might think it, but I ain't. It's just metabolism and will power. Now, Jane Fonda was bulimic. And look where it got her."

"If I can't have a marshmallow, I want a little parasol. Hey, proprietor, I want a little bumbershoot in my drink."

They were too self-consciously exotic to hold his attention any longer. He left some money and walked out into a startling new mist just as a black BMW with smoked windows was disappearing toward the dairy.

Time to rock and roll, he thought.

17

BOSTON AND PHILADELPHIA ARE IN TWO PLACES AT ONCE

A FOG WAS CREEPING IN, FLOWING HALF WAY UP THE TELE-phone poles and slicing itself to ribbons. It cushioned the sky and hushed the streets, an eerie dirty fog that you didn't see often in L.A. In his childhood he'd walked downhill to school into fogs like this, thick ones up from the harbor where the foghorns bayed forlornly, and his legs had disappeared into it first, then the rest of him would be sucked down into the prickly damp.

The warehouse along the road was a colorless shape through the mists. Even the carnival tents were draining of color, and the big eighteen-wheelers that had looked so garish.

Inside he was full of turmoil, tense and confused and blank as if he had forgotten who he was. Then he focused and the outside world didn't matter at all. He felt the angular object in his jacket pocket, the other one uncomfortable in the small of his back. He'd expected anger, but mostly he was just impatient to get it over.

A kind of unease invested the things around him, as if they'd become other than what they were. The steering wheel might suddenly reveal that it had been a snake all along and writhe away. The tall industrial fireplug looked unfamiliar and threatening. Had it been there when he went into the bar? It wasn't fog at all; it was a strange fear etching his vision, like a fine rain of acid frosting a pane of glass.

A legless man went past on a skateboard, paddling the ground urgently with thick leather staves in his hands, then fading into the mist just as a Coke can flew after him, struck the sidewalk and clattered. An old woman limped after him on an aluminum walker, shaking her fist.

It was time. He reached for the ignition key but cause-and-effect seemed to have gone out of the world. The car lurched away from the curb without ever seeming to start. He passed the legless man, bent forward to flail along faster. Everyone had a mission, Jack Liffey thought.

The carnival site dropped behind, and then he was crossing the concrete river once again, water still running in the central channel. Just upriver a weir dammed the flow shallowly to the full width of the channel, twigs and detritus jutting up over the weir to froth the overflow. Down below, oil-scummed pools lay marooned on the dry flats, and isolated rags of mist hovered over the water. He saw gang tags along the concrete banks but no C60L.

The chain link gate into the dairy yard was open, and in the distance he could see the BMW at the office. He parked diagonally across the gate. Mud sucked at his shoes as he limped across the wasteland. Half way was the slab of a vast foundation and a heap of rotting timbers from whatever the structure had been. Remarkably, it still smelled like cow shit, marinating in the damp.

The fog gathered around him and then shimmered all of a sudden, the air turning strangely molten. Space twittered like aspen leaves. His heart pounded and he whirled around as something grazed his cheek. There was a hiss from the flickering nimbus that surrounded him, a faint close seething like a boiling pot. He reeled back and every atom of his intelligence strained to figure out what was happening. He waved an arm into the aura and felt tickles against his hand, furry bursts of contact. Something nipped at his forehead and he ducked.

Then he saw it plastered to his hand—a termite with iridescent wings. He laughed in relief. He could make them out now, wheeling around, orbiting and milling. He saw an opalescent snow of molted wings at his feet and then he noticed the snow writhing as the wingless bodies crawled across the drifts on their epic trek toward decaying wood.

Circus freaks and legless men and termite clouds and murder—life had taken a strange turn. He brushed irritably at the swarm and stepped out into still air, reestablishing a small sphere of normality. No one had come out of the office, and he saw that he still had the element of surprise.

He winced as his ankle twisted suddenly on uneven ground. The tenderness would be with him for at least a month. He concentrated on the ache to keep his mind from reeling away on other errands.

He slid two sandwich baggies onto his hands and took out the little square Dreyse submariner's pistol, manufactured for the Great War, before wars became so common that they started numbering them. He pulled the magazine out. A *magazine*! the Basic instructor from his own war had bellowed in his ear, Never never a clip! A pistol—never never a gun! He counted rounds, and then checked the chamber. He had three shots. The Ballester-Molina wouldn't have worked, because when that ran out, the whole world knew it. Like any Browning action, the receiver stayed back after the last shot, exposing the barrel so you could swap a fresh magazine in and let the receiver snap home to chamber the first round, all in one fluid motion.

He stopped at the office door, but he couldn't hear anything inside. He turned the knob very slowly, just in case they'd locked themselves in, but he felt the mechanism give all the way. He wondered where they would be in the room. Breathe, exhale, pistol up, and he swung the door hard and felt it crash into something that gave.

"Ow! Goddam!"

Al Squinty Butera turned, rubbing his shoulder, and his eyes fastened on the little pistol. One hand twitched, as if wishing to go for his own weapon, but Jack Liffey could see the whole rig of the shoulder holster hanging off a straight chair across the room.

Bobby Snakeskin O'Connor sat at the desk, doing something Jack Liffey hadn't seen in twenty years. A lid of grass was spread across the black linoleum top of the desk and he was picking out seeds and stems. A tiny joint was going between his knuckles, and the room reeked of dope. When O'Connor recognized the visitor, his jaw dropped comically for an instant before his face hardened up into calculation.

"Over there, Squinty," Jack Liffey said. He wanted them both in a small arc of fire. "Knock knock."

O'Connor settled back and took a hit off his joint to demonstrate his cool.

"Let's get all four of our hands flat on the table."

He couldn't find the cowboy hat anywhere. It seemed to matter for some reason. Butera shuffled behind the desk, wiped a space clean of marijuana shreds and leaned forward on his palms.

"Don't go hairy-ass apeshit," Bobby O'Connor said, in a throat voice, holding his breath with the smoke.

"We can talk this over." O'Connor was eyeing the plastic bags on Jack Liffey's hands and he wasn't liking them.

So far, Jack Liffey thought, it had been a nicely structured thirty seconds or so and he didn't feel like pushing anything quite yet.

"What makes you think we have anything to talk about?"

"'Cause we got friends with balls the size of a Buick."

"That's exactly the problem," Jack Liffey said. "You guys are part-time help, but there's always the first string. I've got to find a way to get back up the food chain and convince somebody I'm out of it."

"We could promise to pass the news on," Bobby O'Connor said. "You ain't going to be able to cut the deck any deeper."

It was Butera who was the question mark. Jack Liffey had to know more about him. And the whole thing was complicated by the way Butera had manhandled Eleanor Ong, it made revenge a wild card that he had to fight against.

"We're gonna play a little You Bet Your Life," Jack Liffey said. "Squinty first. Pay attention. Groucho never played it this way, and there's no fuckin' bird with twenty-five dollars gonna drop down. Whether you live or die depends on your answer to one question. Ready? A woman gets in her Volvo and drives from Boston to Philadelphia at forty miles an hour. Then she turns around and drives back at fifty miles an hour. What's her average speed?"

"What the *shit* is this?" It was Bobby O'Connor, rising up out of his chair. "You're plumb loco."

Jack Liffey brought the pistol up and aimed it at the

Cowboy's left eye, the good one, he was sure now. O'Connor puffed once and then subsided.

"Come on, Squinty. I think you heard all the elements. This is the Big S.A.T. You pass and you get another thirty years to live."

Al Butera lifted his head. "Forty-five miles an hour, the average speed is forty-five."

Jack Liffey nodded. "Not bad. Not *right*, but not bad for a guy makes his living the way you do."

"Bullshit!"

"Can you correct him, Snakeskin?"

O'Connor just glared.

"It's a trick question, fellas. You don't have enough information. You see, when she's doing forty from Boston to Philadelphia it takes her longer to make the trip than when she's going back at fifty. So she drives a little longer at forty than at fifty and her average speed is gonna be under forty-five. But I give you a B plus. You got the basic concept of average."

Jack Liffey turned to Bobby O'Connor, whose face was hardening up again. "Where's your hat, Snakeskin?"

"None of your beeswax."

"If that'd been the question, you'd've just flunked, wouldn't you?"

Jack Liffey was astonished that he was carrying it off. Something inside him was running on freewheeling.

"Here's your Groucho question, Snakeskin. Boston and Philadelphia—if they can be in two places at once, how come *you* can't be in two places at once?"

"Fuck you."

Jack Liffey uttered a honk. "*Wrong*. You should never have messed with me, or the woman." For some reason he wouldn't use her name in their presence, it would have been like sullying her. "You could have done your job without messing with us."

The Cowboy's good eye was getting skittish. "Hey, man, I never got a clean shot here."

"Sure you do," Jack Liffey said, even noticing the pun, and he shot the Cowboy three times. The first was in the head and messy, causing a blood-curdling shriek that rang up through the flat hard planes of the room. The next shot may have been in the head, too, because it cut off the noise. The third probably missed entirely as he was collapsing like a sack.

Al Butera had backed away to the wall. He was looking longingly at his shoulder holster.

"Don't think about anything but me and staying alive," Jack Liffey said. He found he was breathing far too fast and he tried to slow himself down. Light swam through the room, and a moment of dizziness came and went.

"Jesus, you just shot him down like a dog. Jesus."

"I chose you because I think you're smart enough to bring this off, but not so smart you feel you have to outwit me. Here."

Jack Liffey lobbed the Dreyse at Al Butera and the man, startled, caught it in both hands. He fumbled it around and found out right away it was empty. By that time, Jack Liffey had his .45 out.

"You see what I mean. Now you've got your prints all over it. You got a family, kids? Put the pistol on the table. *Do it now.*"

"I got no family no more." He leaned in to set the pistol down gingerly, his eyes radaring around to get a glimpse of the Cowboy on the far side. "*Jesus.*"

"I'm gonna cut you loose." Jack Liffey fought a drowsiness that threatened to knock him right off his feet. "Just give me your full attention. Forget your pal, forget your gun, forget what *you* want. This is a mess, but together we're gonna get over. Where you from?"

"Huh?"

Jack Liffey picked up the Dreyse with his baggie and slipped it into his pocket. "Where were you born?"

"Vegas."

"I didn't think anybody was born there. I thought Vegas was a place people went."

"My dad was in security."

"You mean skimming."

"I don't know nothing about that."

"I think maybe I saved the right guy. Now, listen up. You're gonna go back to the guy you work for and convince him I'm out of it. I don't care how you do it. You can say you had some trouble with a guy but he's sleeping in the river. Whatever. I'm out of it, my friends are out of it. We'll never hear from each other again."

Al Butera just stared back heavily, squinching his eyes regularly.

"Because if anything happens to me or my friends, anything at all, this gun is going to the police with a big tag on it saying, I belong to Al Squinty Butera of Las Vegas. And your prints are all over it."

"Man, this is tough."

"It's a lot better odds than you gave me."

He scowled down at his hands. "I don't know what to tell them."

"You've got a better sense of the big picture than me. You know who's in charge, you know what it's all about. Believe it or not, I haven't got a clue and I don't want to know. Your pals can't help you out of this one because your pals don't know where this gun is going to be. This is between you and me, not you and me and Vegas. You're on your own. You know, that's what America's all about, Squinty. Rugged individualism."

Jack Liffey was getting tired of sounding like he was on top of things. It took a lot of effort and he was getting sleepier and sleepier.

"Don't make me think I'd be better off canceling your ticket, too. It's still a possibility."

Al Butera raised both palms. "I'll think of something."

"Good. Now you can walk out into the middle of the field there. You come back when I'm gone and do whatever you feel you have to. You can even dump your pal down the same hole where you put me for all I care. He'll turn up one way or another. Beat it now."

Al Butera didn't even look back. He waddled heavily down the two steps and then walked out into the desolate mudflat.

"Count two hundred steps," Jack Liffey called. "Then you can stop."

He looked over the office quickly but there was nothing of him there. Around the corner of the desk, he saw a motionless gray hand, cupped toward the ceiling. There was a dark pool that looked like chocolate pudding gelling up. Okay, Bobby O'Connor, he thought. You're the guy who killed Consuela Beltran, and God knows who else. The courts do not have a monopoly of justice.

For some reason he felt a wrenching nausea, as if he'd just betrayed someone he loved. Outside, Al Butera was a tiny figure in the wastes, still walking, and Jack Liffey headed for his car.

18

A LOOSE END

A ROLLING MOP CART WAS ON THE LANDING OUTSIDE HIS office, where it shouldn't have been, and it gave him a chill. He stared at it from down below for a while and then hobbled up the steps anyway. By all rights, he'd used up his share of surprises.

From the dairy, he'd gone straight to the big mail terminal at Florence and Central, where the Goodyear plant had once stood, and mailed the Dreyse to Art Castro's private box. He'd run the car through a car wash on general principles—it was good to get anything at all clean—and then he'd parked on the far edge of a supermarket lot and slept fitfully for fifteen minutes. Now he felt just as bad, but he wasn't as sleepy. The three bullets had kicked something loose in his psyche. In fact he felt so bad it gave him a curious sense of invulnerability—the feeling that he was so far gone now he didn't give a damn. It was a dangerous way to be, but he didn't know what to do about it.

"You shouldn't be doing this, Marlena."

"Somebody got to give a hand."

She'd transported the litter of papers from the floor into irregular piles on the desk and credenza, and she was mopping down the scarred green linoleum.

He felt a wave of affection toward the large rump in the tight black skirt that was bent over in front of him, but he refrained from patting it as he went past.

"I didn't try to put nothing away, just get it up."

"Thanks. This is above and beyond the call."

"You ever find out what happened to that woman?"

For just an instant he wondered whether someone had set her to asking. This is what it meant to cross the line, he thought: there was no longer any trust, no longer peace. He took off the shoulder holster, then he hunted around and found the *Oxford Companion to English Literature* and put the .45 inside.

"I think it had to do with gambling and guys with Italian names. I'll never be able to touch them."

"They did this mess, too?"

"Probably."

"And your ankles?"

It took him only an instant. "Nah. That was clumsiness. I've always had weak ankles." Don't beat it to death, he thought. Just let it lie. He figured he ought to get a rag off the mop cart and make a show of helping, so he hobbled to the door.

"You're not going to do nothing?"

"I can't fight Al Capone."

From the landing he saw the car pull up below. It was one of the Cahuenga cop cars with the beige stripe, the designer police straight out of the barrio.

Even foreshortened down there he recognized Zuniga and Millan as they got out. Lieutenant Zuniga looked up and saw him. The big cop raised a hand overhead and made a little arcing stab motion that seemed to be telling him to stay put.

"Marlena, I think I've got guests."

She planted the string mop in the pail and looked over the railing.

"They're cops," he said.

"Catch me later, *querido*. I gotta sort the mail." She kissed his cheek and her voice got husky. "I wanna rub a part of you against Brown Betty."

That gave him a little charge, but he didn't have time to think about it. Lieutenant Zuniga came up first, eyeing Marlena suspiciously as he passed. Sergeant Millan was puffing badly after only the first flight, halted on the landing with his face going florid.

They went in and Lieutenant Zuniga didn't seem surprised.

"Things are bit messy just now," Jack Liffey said. He thought of asking why they had left their jurisdiction, but they would tell him, or they wouldn't.

"I hear a couple guys from Vegas did this." Zuniga prowled around, poking at the piles of papers and folders. "It's a definite rumor," he added. "You've come to be a real rock in our shoe on this Beltran matter."

The brown eyes rested on him thoughtfully. Sergeant Millan came in at last and sat in the stiff chair, trying to catch his breath. Jack Liffey wondered if Cahuenga P.D. required a physical for requalifying. Millan would never make it.

"You got those uh-oh eyes," Zuniga said.

"It's just my normal sense of remorse at life."

"I hear you shot up their car pretty good. It's amazing how much of this stuff is just plain dis getting out of hand. They come in and disrespect you and you got to go over and dis them back. Life is getting to be like the McCoys and the Whatevers."

"Don't tell me you're gonna bust me for assassinating a couple of radial tires?"

Lieutenant Zuniga shrugged. "Nobody ever signed a

complaint. A secretary at a mortgage broker gave a pretty good description of you, though.''

"I did it, sure. It was a .38 I took off one of the kids, and I just blew my cool. Afterward I threw it in the river. You're right, those guys got in my face, and then I had to get in theirs. It was stupid, but luckily that was the end of it. It's their turn to come after me, and they haven't.''

Lieutenant Zuniga just stared. Sergeant Millan finally caught his breath and came up straight in the chair. "What a line of shit. We know you were at the dairy. And we know you're the one that capped that cowboy asshole.''

"What?''

"Nice try, not bad," Millan said. "Surprise is a little more open mouth, though, more eyebrows, loosen up your hands. You been watchin' too much Clint Eastwood, with all that *under*play." Millan sat back and cocked his head. "You ever see the one, he takes over a whole fuckin' Montana town, jumps their women, makes 'em come across with new clothes, then makes 'em paint the whole place red, the whole town? Never cracks a smile. That's what I call chutzpah.''

"*High Plains Drifter,*" Jack Liffey said. He wasn't sure Millan would pass the IQ test on the re-up, either.

"Sure, whatever." Sergeant Millan seemed to catch a look from his partner and wound down.

"We know the Cowboy was a scumbag," Lieutenant Zuniga said. "Probably killed Mrs. Beltran, probably would of got away with it. And that dope-dealer's Beemer deserves whatever wrecking it gets, no trouble there. What hurts us is the way you made so much *disarray*. Christ on a crutch, how you had the stomach for it. The human body is the temple of the spirit, you know. Looks like you cut the Cowboy's head open with a pair of pinking shears.''

''What?'' Jack Liffey felt a chill.

''That was better,'' Sergeant Millan put in, then subsided when the lieutenant glared at him.

''What'd you think, we're too stupid to get you if you cut him open and retrieve your bullets? That just disses *us*, you know? We got the best case-clear record on major crimes in the east county. Besides you forgot the slug in the two-by-four in the wall, hardly hit him. Must have gone right through the fleshy part of the neck. Marks on it are real clear.''

Jack Liffey said nothing. Had Butera actually dug the spent bullets out of his partner's head? It was a gruesome angle he hadn't figured at all.

''You're under arrest for murder, Mr. Liffey.''

His mind ran a mile a minute while they were explaining his rights and handcuffing him and poking around the office. He hadn't been so clever after all.

''My piece is in that big blue book,'' he said. ''You'll want to check that. And the overalls with all the blood on them are in my car.''

A hand closed on his upper arm, harder than necessary. ''Don't be a wise guy. It's not worth it. We want permission to look around your house.''

''Only if you'll cut me loose right away if you don't find anything.''

''I guess we get a warrant.''

THERE was no comfortable way to sit in the car with his hands cuffed behind him. He pulled his wrists off center and watched neutrally out the window.

''El-tee, you see that episode of *Cops* last night?'' Sergeant Millan asked. Lieutenant Zuniga was driving. ''The one they stop the guy and he stands there, grabs his Johnson like some colored rapper and gets in their face. They bleep a whole fifteen seconds of his mouth. Somewhere in Kansas, I think.''

"Nah. I don't watch it any more.''

They came to a stop behind a clot of cars filling a residential street. Lieutenant Zuniga honked once. Something was going on in front of a house.

"There's like this cutaway. Another car arrives or something and when they're back, the guy's gone through a whole attitude adjustment, he's real pleasant to everybody, only he's got blood on his lip.'' He laughed. "Man, I'd like to see the stuff they cut out.''

"You got to know they edit the shit out of it.''

"Yeah, the people hit the cops, but the cops never hit the people.''

Lieutenant Zuniga honked harder and craned his neck. Finally the oncoming lane cleared so he could pull around. Then he slammed on the brakes. Between stopped cars, Jack Liffey could see a Jeep Cherokee with its doors open up on the lawn, a big guy with a hacksaw engaged in cutting the station wagon in two. He was already through the roof and making headway on the rocker panel under the rear door. The hacksaw made a terrible noise.

"What the hell . . . ?''

Lieutenant Zuniga got out and called to the hacksaw man. "Hey, partner, you got the paper on that car?''

The guy looked up, his eyes inflamed. "Who the fuck wants to know?''

"Police,'' Lieutenant Zuniga said mildly.

"I paid *cash* this useless sonabitch, *cash* up front, and three times it stops in the fuckin' middle of the freeway, jams up the brakes, turns on all the alarms and horns and leaves me there with my thumb up my ass and people pointing at me, and the dealership won't do nothing, say they can't find nothing wrong—''

''Go right ahead, sir. It's your property. *The rest of you move out!*''

He climbed back in the car.

''Out of our jurisdiction anyway.''

The hacksaw noise started in again. Zuniga gave a little squirt of his siren as he drove past, but nobody seemed to be clearing away.

At last Jack Liffey's mind settled enough to look at his situation calmly. He was lucky they'd found the third bullet. Nothing had changed, really. All he had to do was make sure Al Butera knew the cops had it, and that he still wasn't off the hook, despite all his unpleasant surgery.

''You think the world's getting worse?'' Sergeant Millan said. ''Stuff like that, I dunno. Everybody's angry, everybody's got a *grievance* they can't put their finger on. I mean, hell, I got a house and two cars and a boat and *I* feel that way. It's like some *disease* of anger settled over us, coast to coast.''

He looked around at Jack Liffey, as if just remembering he was there. ''Citizen like this, looks calm on the surface but he's a mass of raw nerves. Ain't you?''

''You guys get your hair cut by the Marines down in Pendleton?''

Sergeant Millan glared, then laughed suddenly. ''See what I mean? It's off the high side.''

For a moment Jack Liffey wondered if Millan was right. It seemed a sure bet that the world was in decline, but maybe the sense of decay was just an illusion, no different from all those fine hopes of the 1950s that things were getting better and better all the time, just motoring smoothly up the on-ramp of History. Some things got better and some got worse and it was a kind

of megalomania to think there was an overall pattern.
All you had was your way of judging each thing. You
couldn't let go of that.

They interrogated him for hours in a barren little
room and he stuck to the story he and Eleanor had come
up with. She'd fallen into the channel one night, and he
had hurt himself dragging her out. Beyond that, he'd
never been to the dairy and he hadn't seen the cowboy
and his pal after shooting up their car. It wasn't too hard
as long as he resisted the urge to embellish or give them
a little lip. Curiously, things had become disconnected
in his head and made it all easier. He had come to feel
that the core of the crime was digging the bullets out of
the cowboy's head, and since he hadn't done that, he
could work up a little indignation at his innocence.

They insisted on driving him across town and making
him walk through the dairy, apparently working on some
theory from Police Science 101 about criminals confessing when they had to confront the scene of their
crime. Then he was forced to watch as they turned his
apartment upside down. There was nothing illegal there,
but he hated watching them put their hands on everything. They turned the sofa upside down and prodded
into it with what looked like knitting needles. They
popped open the air conditioner that he'd never used.
Took the grill off the bathroom vent fan. Unrolled all
his socks and fondled his underwear. It felt like a massive violation.

Everything was left in a mess, and finally they threatened him again, half-heartedly, and drove off. He'd
never actually been booked. It had all been a con to scare
him.

It didn't even make him angry, his thoughts were so
dulled and ponderous. Passion had gone out of him.
Would it leak back in through Eleanor? That's probably

what she meant to him, a kind of access to whatever it was he had lost somewhere. He longed to see her.

But now he had to let Squinty Butera know that the cops had the third bullet. How? He remembered the note from his office door, with the letter S or maybe a snake and a phone number. It seemed like weeks ago, but it had only been three days. He went through the mess of his condo looking for the note, took over an hour making the mess worse, then trooped back to his office and dug methodically down through Marlena's tidying. He found it at last, a yellow Post-it stuck to an unpaid phone bill that must have been near the phone when he called, another mark of letting himself get distracted. He went to a phone booth outside a 7-Eleven.

"Yeah?" said a voice darkly, after eight rings. It wasn't Butera. A truck rumbled past and he waited for the noise to fade down.

"This is a message for the guy with the squint."

"Nobody like that here."

"Look, we're way past that. This is as straightforward as it's gonna get. The third one went into the wall and the police have it. The deal stands. Bye-bye now." He had no taste for trading threats so he hung up. He waited, staring at his trembling hand on the receiver. He wondered how long he was going to have to watch his back.

19

SILENCE

A BATTERED CROWN VICTORIA WITH SONORA PLATES WAS
backed up on the lawn between the courts, all its doors
open, and the whole neighborhood was helping empty
out House B. There was a pyramid of cartons behind
the car, and the big furniture was at the curb. Two men
were lashing the kitchen table into a pickup and an old
woman clutched an armful of dresses and scurried away
as if someone might ask for them back.

Everything in Jack Liffey's life seemed to be
mounded up haphazardly—the contents of his office, his
condo, and now the last will and testament of Consuela
Beltran. Senora Schuler stood over the cartons, selecting
items to jigsaw into the crowded rear seat, a small brown
determined woman building something to last. There
was no reason, he thought, that an Indian woman packing a horse and travois for a cross-country migration
should appear any more courageous or dignified.

Tony and his friends lounged by a Chevy that had
been chopped and lowered into a platinum teardrop.
Two older boys sat inside the car, and Tony's homemade
bar bells stuck out of the trunk.

''T-Bell,'' Jack Liffey called.

"Hey, Mr. Liffey." The boy sauntered across the grass.

"Where you going?"

"Mexico," he said glumly. "Grandma taking me to her place in Hermosillo."

"Have you ever been there?"

"I never been 'crost at all. Nabo says my Spanish sucks. If I say *el churcho* and *el carro* they gonna laugh at me in real Mexico."

"There's nothing second-rate about being from California. You just tell them that's where Ritchie Valens came from. I want to speak to you and your grandma."

"Sure, okay." As they walked toward the car, the boy reached up shyly and touched Jack Liffey's arm through the shirt, just where his tattoo was. "Did you kill a lot of people in the war?"

"I didn't kill anybody. I usually left my M-16 in the barracks."

"You didn't never fight?"

"I was in Saigon for Tet and I got caught in an attack, but I didn't do much. I shot up a lot of concrete but I don't think I hit anybody."

Would it all have been easier if he *had* seen combat? He'd known enough guys who could kill without scruple and never get a sleepless minute from it. He wondered what it was like to be that way. And if it made things easier, what did you lose in the bargain?

"Abuela . . ."

She seemed genuinely pleased to see Jack Liffey, and she started talking so fast that Tony had to stop her to translate.

"She tried to call to tell you we are going but your telephone machine is not working."

The cops probably had the cassette. It was in some forensic lab with overheated amps working overtime to reconstitute the faint tonalities of Kathy's lament about child support.

"She says . . . it's hard to translate. Because she met you, she doesn't think so bad of America."

He nodded. "Thank you." He waited while a man in a strap undershirt deposited a glass bowl and moved off. There was no one else around all of a sudden. "Please tell her that what I'm going to say right now is just for you two. No one else." He owed them something.

She nodded gravely.

"Your mother was murdered. The man who did it has paid. He's dead now. You must never ask what happened." He didn't explain that the man who gave the orders for it was still around somewhere, and no one would ever hold his kind to account.

The boy repeated enthusiastically and a lot of emotions passed over the woman's face as she listened. Then a tension seemed to go out of her and her shoulders sagged. She sat on the edge of the back seat and wept.

"Was it the man with the cowboy boots?" the boy whispered eagerly. "Did you kill him?"

Jack Liffey made a hushing gesture. "It's our secret, *compañero*." He tucked his business card into the breast pocket of the boy's white T-shirt. "Call me when you get back up here some day and I'll buy you lunch. Maybe we can go look at some airplanes."

The boy smiled. "I remember the B-29 at that place. You showed me the bomb doors and told me about the little boy they dropped on Hiroshima."

The Little Boy dropped on Hiroshima was the first bomb, the one made from Uranium 235. What did they call the one that had dropped on his life?

Suddenly Tony bolted for the house, and then he came back dragging the mangy white coyote on a rope.

The dog resisted by getting sideways, then having itself yanked around.

''Please, would you take Loco? Abuela says he can't come to Hermosillo.''

Just what he needed. The dog glared at him and stood his ground. It should have looked intelligent. It had the forehead break of a collie or shepherd, but the eyes were too flat and dry. There didn't seem to be any curiosity behind them.

''Loco, huh?''

The boy grinned, and Jack Liffey took the rope.

''*Vaya con dios*, Tony. Be hopeful.''

HIS own dullness began to shift as he drove, and some strange emotion was inside him all of a sudden, banging around like a rat in a wastebasket. Feelings darted up and stuck out their tongues. Shame, disgrace, plain dread. A primitive kind of scruple had been blasted away with his three shots. He'd killed in cold blood.

Most of his life he had tried to behave in ways that he would not mind answering for. Now he had done something that put him beyond the marker, into a place where he had to admit that he could do the same things that the men in prisons did. He was the same human species as serial killers and child molesters. It made him queasy, and he wished he had his old aerospace job back.

Loco made a mewling sound now and again. The dog had curled up on the rear floor, trying to pretend it was somewhere else. Loco obviously didn't like cars much.

The Harbor Freeway was blocked by cop cars just past Martin Luther King, and the whole northbound was diverted onto the surface. People fumed and honked. One guy with a pony tail was bobbing up and down with such frustration that his Lexus rocked with it. Nine-

year-olds darted among the stopped cars banging on
bumpers with sticks and taunting the drivers. It looked
like an organized game. When he finally got back on at
Exposition it was like the start of the Indy. He glanced
back down the empty freeway to see yellow crime-scene
tape and, beyond it, two horses lying on their sides in a
big pool of blood. He didn't see a horse trailer anywhere.

HE peeked in through the little glass window in the door,
like checking out a nocturnal cage at the zoo to see if
the bushbaby was interesting enough to bother. She was
out of traction, lying on her side on top of the covers to
read a magazine, and he felt himself flooding with tenderness. He wondered what the magazine was. *Hair
Shirt? Nun's Digest?*

It was a double room, with the other bed mussed but
vacant. He wondered if there was any way on earth he
could make love to her right there. Paint out the little
window, jam the door. . . . Just the thought aroused him
as he pushed in.

She jumped a little, startled. "Oh, hi."

"I love your leg warmers. You're going to start a
whole new plaster of paris fad."

There was something nervous and aloof about her
eyes that he didn't like.

"It's no picnic."

"William Holden and Kim Novak."

"Huh?"

"Never mind."

She readjusted and he saw that the magazine was
something called *Commonweal*. It didn't look like the
kind of journal that told you handy hints for homemak-
ing.

"Where's your cell-mate?"

She glanced over at the mussed bed. "She's in surgery. Would you fix the blinds?"

The sun had come out and bright stripes slashed her face. He torqued his body around behind the mussed bed to get at the controls.

"Happy?"

"Thanks." She was still squinting against the brightness, and, unobserved, he ran a mental fingertip over the planes of her face. He liked the idea.

"I missed you," he said.

She nodded but didn't respond, and he sat on the side of the bed and touched her shoulder. "What's the matter?"

It took her a while to start. "I'm in a foreign country, Jack. I don't speak the language very well."

Her tone hadn't been plaintive, just sad and resolved and a bit hasty, like someone who had taken a week working up to her confession and had to get to a priest before she backed down. His mind flashed forward, intuition working overtime, and he thought he took in her full drift in an instant, his insides knotting up with it. But he knew he would refuse to acknowledge anything until she spelled it out.

"Go on."

She looked into his eyes.

"When we make love, do you ever think of another woman?"

He shook his head. "I don't think people do that very much. You may be thinking of yourself and fixating on your own pleasure, but most sex is pretty real. Unreality just gets in the way."

"Jack, I think of Jesus," she said. "I can't help it."

"Uh-oh."

"I'm not really at home out here. I didn't bargain for any of this." She indicated the casts. "It scares me to death. Even ordinary things. It's been bothering me for a long time. I was the quiet kid at home, off in my room painting or reading. But no matter where I was, Dad was there somewhere arching over me. Even in the convent, I think. When he died last year, I became a lot smaller and the world became more frightening.

"I think I've got a sort of agoraphobia of the spirit. It's been harder than I thought to leave the asylum of the Church. I'm not strong enough."

"We all want to run back to our parents sometimes. Especially after we've had a good fright. *I'm* scared, too, but the worst is over. We got through it."

She stared at her hands but she wouldn't let him budge her.

"You've got a whole community at the House to lean on," he said. "You've got me." He sensed the desperate tone creeping into his voice.

She took his hand, but wouldn't look up at him. "I don't think I want people that close to me. I want to go back into my room. It's hard to face, but I think my vocation is for something more private. I'm going to the convent."

"You're just scared. I've seen it before, *really*."

She met his eyes finally and her face softened, grew panicky and then went blank. She'd got past some critical internal checkpoint and it was downhill now.

"I've fallen in love with you," he insisted. "I want to protect you."

Then she brought him to a dead stop. Her voice came to him in a beatific, forgiving, thousand-mile-away voice, repeating words from another life. "Jack, I don't think you're going to make it."

A chill took him and his mind reeled. What did she mean? But he knew what she meant, he just didn't have enough confidence left to answer it. He argued for a while, watching the stillness and serenity grow over her like a shell of steel. She pulled farther and farther from him, withdrawing above the clouds into her cuckoo realm, a place he would never know and never honor. He felt a hollowness open inside himself.

"Look, I'm not a big player, Eleanor. I never have been. I just hoe my garden, and I take care of my own. I wouldn't let you down."

"I don't mind that, Jack. I just don't know the rules out here, and what I know, I don't like. I think I have a . . . religious temperament. We call it a vocation. I shouldn't have tried to turn my back on it."

"So you're going to deny the rest of yourself and the rest of us? You're a really loving person."

She just smiled with her new Buddha smile, and he knew she was lost. Okay, he thought—this could be the gift he gave her. And after all, she would be safer in cloud cuckooland, away from the Cowboy's friends. "Can I still see you?"

"Jack. Please. Soon I'm going to be silent."

"You mean one of those places where nobody ever talks? Oh, shit."

"I need inner peace. Please."

"We'll never talk again?" He was chilled to the bone.

"I mean 'never' now, Jack, I'm sorry, but only God owns the real 'never.' Who knows?"

He lay his palm on her wrist, but there was no response. "You know, life will be over soon enough," he said with an edge, but then he dropped it. "Sorry, you do what you have to. Bye, kid."

As he was leaving, he thought he heard a few soft words from her. It might have been a blessing, but that only counted if you believed in it.

●　　●　　●

THE dog had come over into the front seat and had its nose to the glass.

"Back off," Jack Liffey said as he got in.

He decided a smoke and a drink would be a hell of a good idea. He bought a box of Shermans and a quart of single malt and carried them in a brown bag up into the derelict oil fields of the Baldwin Hills overlooking Culver City. There was a slit in the chain link fence and he pulled it open like a vagina and pushed Loco through, then followed. They strolled along a dirt road between oil pumps that no longer pumped, though a few others high on the hillsides above the path, maybe one in ten, still thrummed and grunted as they bobbed away. A sign on the fence around a well pump said, *Danger: this machinery starts automatically*, but he didn't believe it.

A rabbit hurried away clumsily and Loco's rope went taut. The dog didn't bark. Maybe he had too much dignity. It wasn't a jackrabbit, but a short-eared gray rabbit of some kind, and it tucked behind a tall castor bean with elephant-ear leaves. A pair of cross-country runners passed, huffing along the trail to give Loco a wide berth and they nodded, drenched with sweat.

Jack Liffey led the dog off the jeep road and climbed a weedy hillside until he could look out over Culver City. He could see his condo complex below, his own unit obscured by a stand of eucalyptus. He lit a long thin Sherman and decapped the Scotch and drank straight from the bottle. A sacrilege with single malt, but he was feeling particularly sacrilegious. In fact, you could put all religions in a sack and sink it out past the three-mile limit, particularly Catholicism. He tried cursing religion for a while, but it didn't make him feel any better.

He fed the dog peanut-butter crackers, the only treat in the liquor store that it looked like a dog might like. It did.

Smoke rose off a factory building and he heard the faint sirens, then saw the fire engines approaching. Burn, baby, burn. The wail seemed to affect Loco and Liffey stroked its chest again, both of them seeming to gather calm from it.

Jack Liffey remembered looking out over L.A. in April 1992 with a profound sense of unease as roving gangs torched department stores and Korean mini-malls, and pillars of dark smoke rose all around the horizon, like burnt offerings to malign gods. Back then he'd finally located the unease: his sense of a world that was steadily getting worse, and nobody gave a damn, nobody was putting anything but token effort into fixing things, as a sort of social entropy carried the whole country down into chaos. The poor suffered, the rulers turned their backs and the rich retreated into armed enclaves.

He heard a crashing of brush below and hunted for the cause. A muscled wiry kid strolling down the path flailed absent-mindedly with a nunchak to decapitate castor beans and tree tobacco and young sumac as he passed. There it was, he thought, a coded portrait of his world—the random reaper. He liked the sound of the words and he said "the random reaper" aloud a few times as he drank. Loco sat against him and nuzzled his leg.

He noticed the bottle was half empty. Then, with the pressure against his leg, he experienced a flush of sexuality and thought about Marlena Cruz. How promiscuous the imagination was, he thought. Only an hour earlier he'd been pleading for Eleanor Ong, and now he wanted Marlena Cruz, thinking about the delicious abandon of her heavy body, the tenderness that would well over him to blot out thoughts of anything else. He looked at the Scotch bottle and decided there was

enough left to introduce her to the peaty glories of unblended.

"Loco, want to eat a lapdog?"

HER car was there. He parked at the corner and left Loco
in the back sleeping. He felt rain as he approached her
door and glared suspiciously up at the cloudless blue
sky. It came again, just a teasing on his bare arms. He
glanced down and saw tiny pale spots spreading like
colonies of bacteria on his dark shirt. He watched in
fascination as more dots appeared and groped outward,
then he snapped his head around and caught a glimpse
of the small boy fleeing, a big pump squirt rifle chugging
at his side. Bleach, he thought.

He had hid in the bushes as a child to send a spray
across the windshield of cars stopped at a red light, but
that had been harmless water. It had been one of his
favorite shirts, but no great loss in the run of the universe.

He felt for his key ring. She had given him a key but
he decided to be gentlemanly and knock. A sexual thick-
ness welled in him and he tried out smiles to offer her,
tender greetings. It was a heavy dense door and he
wasn't sure the knock carried, but he waited a few moments before ringing the bell so he wouldn't seem per-
emptory. He could feel the touch of her skin.

He thought he heard a footstep inside, though it might
only have been house noise, one of those creaks caused
by board and batten absorbing heat differentially. He
rapped once more and the door opened a crack. He could
just see her face thrust against the opening.

"Oh."

"Hi, Marlena."

"You should tell me you're coming."

"Sorry. I wasn't near a phone." He felt wronged;

he'd gone out of his way not to open the door with his own key. Something tragic was in her voice and he felt his smile stiffening. She wore a bathrobe, her hand clutching it closed high up at the neck and he reached in slowly to try to slide his hand in at breast level, hoping an intimate touch would reestablish some of his sexual tenderness. But everything was topsy-turvey. She backed away from his hand in a panicky way, pulling the door open farther.

The man stood across the living room, sawing the ends of the tie through his collar. The uniform shirt itself was only half-buttoned.

Jack Liffey found himself blinking a couple of times, as if he could make the terrible apparition go away.

"He was axing about Consuela Beltran," she said, a pretext so lame that the words clogged in her throat. The man whistled to himself, letting his shoulders ripple a little as he fiddled with the tie.

"I'm sure Sergeant Quinn always leaves his shirt over the chair when he conducts police business."

It was the best he could do, short of shooting Quinn.

"You got some sort of trouble, fella?"

"Not with you. Good night, Marlena."

"Jack . . ."

But he was outside, feeling his cheeks on fire. It wasn't even night. Later, he thought, he would laugh at all this, but not now. He clutched the half bottle of unblended Scotch, and when he opened car door, Loco woke with a start and obviously didn't know him. The dog snarled and the two of them sat for a time glaring at one another, yoked together in a silent world.

THE dog gnarred several times as Jack Liffey tugged it across the condo complex, past the scent trails of Persian Cats and German Shepherds and toy poodles. Someone had dumped a big parcel of rags on his doorstep. It sat there in the shadows and the dog hung back instinctively, forelegs stiff. Then he noticed what it was and hid the Scotch bottle behind his back. She was sitting on the rope doormat with her arms clasped around her knees and her head down.

"Honey, what's wrong?"

"Oh, Daddy, I miss you so."

She jumped up and hugged him. Her head only came to his belly, and it rooted against his shirt. In a moment one of her hands accidentally found the bottle and she pulled back.

"You're not drinking again?"

He brought the bottle into plain sight, eyed the label that said twelve years old—three years older than she was—and then decapped it and stuffed it upside down into the dirt of the piggy-back plant. "Maeve, meet Loco."

She and the dog cocked their heads at one another, as if sizing up for a duel.

"What happened to your key?"

"Mom took it. She said I couldn't come over till you pay up. Where'd you get Loco from?"

"My last client had to abandon him. He's half coyote or half Mexican wolf."

With a last disapproving frown at the bottle she took his hand and tugged him inside.

"I'm going to have to call your mom, but maybe she'll let you stay tonight."

"Couldn't you just wait and call her when it's too late to go home?"

Loco sniffed from room to room, half sideways, investigating like a cat.

"She'll be worried, Maeve. We can't do that. Have you eaten?"

"I got a fish sandwich up at Dan's."

"On the cuff?"

"Huh?"

"Did you pay for it?"

"He said you'd be good for it."

"Why don't you set up the board and I'll call."

From the kitchen, as he was calling, he watched the gangly girl bustle away the place settings and hunt in the brown Scrabble box for one particular tile. In her very movements he saw quotes of Kathy's body language, and his own, a way she frowned in concentration, biting her cheek, and a way she held herself stiffly and wriggled one shoulder.

"Hello."

"Kathy, this is Jack. Maeve is here with me."

"Oh, *dammit*, Jack. I was petrified."

"I just got home. She's okay. Couldn't you let her stay for tonight? I know the deal. I think I could come up with one month's child support. I hate to beg, but she really wants to stay."

"You're nine months behind." She paused. He knew she wasn't really a hardass about it, but her lawyer was pushing her.

"The kid went out of her way, and she's setting up Scrabble right now."

"Oh, Jack, you could always talk your way around me."

"No, I couldn't. You saw through me."

"Are you drinking?"

He hesitated. "If she hadn't shown up, I would be. I had a bad day but I'm okay now."

"You'll have her back by noon?"

"I swear it on a stack of Bibles."

As he was waiting for the final okay he put a bowl of water and an old dish of stew on the floor for Loco, and the dog glared at them with black almond-shaped eyes. The dog would have to learn to like table scraps. Life was like that.

"Okay, but I want to talk to you when you drop her off. We've got to get her straight on obeying me."

"I'll talk to her now. Thanks, Kath. You're a princess."

He set the phone down and watched Maeve laboriously turning the tiles blank side up, one by one, as if each required a slightly different manipulation of her wrist. He was amazed at how quickly his mood could shift. From despair and humiliation only a few minutes ago, he was filled with love—and with the anxiety he always felt at her delicacy. Her arms were so frail it looked like the weight of the air in the room was enough to crush them. How would she ever survive adolescence? How did she exist in the same world with the deadly Cowboy and Las Vegas mobsters?

She laughed and stuck out her tongue. "Daddy, you'll never go first. I drew a B."

Never grow up, never grow up, he pleaded. His cheeks burned and then he realized he was crying.

RICHARD BARRE

Winner of the Shamus Award for Best First Novel

"The book's strength comes from the chance it takes."
        —*Chicago Tribune*

There are seven of them. Children—innocents—whose long-buried remains are uncovered by a flash flood. No one knows who could have committed such a crime. Clues are scarce, and with the media turning the story into a law enforcement nightmare, time is short. Only Wil Hardesty, a private eye who has more in common with the case than anyone knows, is willing to push hard enough—and dig deep enough—to find the cruelest of killers. The killer of...

THE INNOCENTS

___0-425-16109-9/$5.99

Look for the Prime Crime hardcover
THE GHOSTS OF MORNING
Coming in June 1998

Payable in U.S. funds. No cash accepted. Postage & handling: $1.75 for one book, 75¢ for each additional. Maximum postage $5.50. Prices, postage and handling charges may change without notice. Visa, Amex, MasterCard call 1-800-788-6262, ext. 1, or fax 1-201-933-2316; refer to ad #772

Or, check above books	Bill my: ☐ Visa ☐ MasterCard ☐ Amex _____ (expires)

and send this order form to:
The Berkley Publishing Group   Card#_____

P.O. Box 12289, Dept. B   Daytime Phone #_____   ($10 minimum)
Newark, NJ 07101-5289   Signature_____

Please allow 4-6 weeks for delivery.   Or enclosed is my: ☐ check ☐ money order
Foreign and Canadian delivery 8-12 weeks.

Ship to:

Name_____   Book Total $_____
Address_____   Applicable Sales Tax $_____
                                        (NY, NJ, PA, CA, GST Can.)
City_____   Postage & Handling $_____
State/ZIP_____   Total Amount Due $_____

Bill to: Name_____
Address_____   City_____
State/ZIP_____

"Sharp and jolly...There's a lot to enjoy."—*Chicago Tribune*

TONY DUNBAR

New Mysteries starring:

TUBBY DUBONNET

"Reminiscent of...Elmore Leonard."—*Booklist*

CROOKED MAN
___0-425-15138-7/$4.99

New Orleans lawyer Tubby Dubonnet always does his best for his client, whether it's the doctor who refers patients to Tubby for malpractice suits or the man who drives a Mardi Gras float shaped like a giant crawfish pot. But Tubby's newest client was busted in a drug deal. He hid his money—almost a million dollars—in Tubby's office. Then he got murdered.

CITY OF BEADS
___0-425-15578-1/$5.99

Tubby is growing less excited about life as a lawyer. Until he starts working for his newest client—a very lucrative casino run by some very shady characters. Suddenly Tubby is doing something different and exciting—he's running for his life...

Payable in U.S. funds. No cash accepted. Postage & handling: $1.75 for one book, 75¢ for each additional. Maximum postage $5.50. Prices, postage and handling charges may change without notice. Visa, Amex, MasterCard call 1-800-788-6262, ext. 1, or fax 1-201-933-2316; refer to ad #756

Or, check above books   Bill my: ☐ Visa ☐ MasterCard ☐ Amex _____ (expires)
and send this order form to:
The Berkley Publishing Group   Card#_____
P.O. Box 12289, Dept. B   Daytime Phone #_____ ($10 minimum)
Newark, NJ 07101-5289   Signature_____
Please allow 4-6 weeks for delivery.   Or enclosed is my: ☐ check ☐ money order
Foreign and Canadian delivery 8-12 weeks.

Ship to:

Name_____	Book Total $_____
Address_____	Applicable Sales Tax $_____ (NY, NJ, PA, CA, GST Can.)
City_____	Postage & Handling $_____
State/ZIP_____	Total Amount Due $_____

Bill to: Name_____

Address_____City_____
State/ZIP_____

B. B. Jordan

PRINCIPAL
Investigation

A Scientific Mystery

One man holds the cure to a mutant strain of the Eke virus—one of the most deadly of all. And for the sake of money and power, he's holding the whole world hostage. But there's an even greater problem:

No one knows if the cure will work.

Now virologist Dr. Celeste Braun must turn her scientific skills to the art of investigation—by solving the crime and finding the cure...

__0-425-16090-4/$5.99

Payable in U.S. funds. No cash accepted. Postage & handling: $1.75 for one book, 75¢ for each additional. Maximum postage $5.50. Prices, postage and handling charges may change without notice. Visa, Amex, MasterCard call 1-800-788-6262, ext. 1, or fax 1-201-933-2316; refer to ad #755

Or, check above books and send this order form to:	Bill my: ☐ Visa ☐ MasterCard ☐ Amex _____ (expires)
The Berkley Publishing Group	Card#_____
P.O. Box 12289, Dept. B	Daytime Phone #_____ ($10 minimum)
Newark, NJ 07101-5289	Signature_____
Please allow 4-6 weeks for delivery.	Or enclosed is my: ☐ check ☐ money order
Foreign and Canadian delivery 8-12 weeks.	

Ship to:

Name_____	Book Total	$_____
Address_____	Applicable Sales Tax (NY, NJ, PA, CA, GST Can.)	$_____
City_____	Postage & Handling	$_____
State/ZIP_____	Total Amount Due	$_____

Bill to: Name_____

Address_____ City_____

State/ZIP_____

Gary Phillips

PERDITION, U.S.A.

When three young black men are gunned down
within blocks of one another, Ivan Monk investi-
gates for a possible link—and finds himself on the
trail of a racial conspiracy centered in a small
Northwestern town.

__0-425-15900-0/$5.99

VIOLENT SPRING

The body of a murdered Korean liquor store owner
is unearthed during a groundbreaking ceremony
at the infamous intersection of Florence and
Normandie. As racial tensions increase, black private eye Ivan Monk searches for the killer.

__0-425-15625-7/$5.99

Payable in U.S. funds. No cash accepted. Postage & handling: $1.75 for one book, 75¢ for each
additional. Maximum postage $5.50. Prices, postage and handling charges may change without
notice. Visa, Amex, MasterCard call 1-800-788-6262, ext. 1, or fax 1-201-933-2316; refer to ad # 732

Or, check above books	Bill my: ☐ Visa	☐ MasterCard	☐ Amex _____ (expires)

and send this order form to:
The Berkley Publishing Group   Card#_____

P.O. Box 12289, Dept. B   Daytime Phone #_____

Newark, NJ 07101-5289   Signature_____

Please allow 4-6 weeks for delivery.   **Or enclosed is my:** ☐ check ☐ money order

Foreign and Canadian delivery 8-12 weeks.

Ship to:

Name_____   Book Total $_____

Address_____   Applicable Sales Tax $_____
(NY, NJ, PA, CA, GST Can.)

City_____   Postage & Handling $_____

State/ZIP_____   Total Amount Due $_____

Bill to: Name_____

Address_____City_____

State/ZIP_____